UTZ

UTZ

Bruce Chatwin

VIKING

VIKING
Published by the Penguin Group
Viking Penguin Inc., 40 West 23rd Street,
New York, New York 10010, U.S.A.
Penguin Books Ltd, 27 Wrights Lane,
London W8 5TZ, England
Penguin Books Australia Ltd, Ringwood,
Victoria, Australia
Penguin Books Canada Ltd, 2801 John Street,
Markham, Ontario, Canada L3R 1B4
Penguin Books (N.Z.) Ltd, 182–190 Wairau Road,
Auckland 10, New Zealand

Penguin Books Ltd, Registered Offices:
Harmondsworth, Middlesex, England

First American Edition
Published in 1989 by Viking Penguin Inc.

1   3   5   7   9   10   8   6   4   2

LIBRARY OF CONGRESS CATALOGING IN PUBLICATION DATA
Chatwin, Bruce.
Utz.
I. Title.
PR6053.H395U8   1989   823'.914   88-40310
ISBN 0-670-82497-6

Printed in the United States of America by
Arcata Graphics, Fairfield, Pennsylvania
Set in Bodoni

For Diana Phipps

UTZ

An hour before dawn on March 7th 1974, Kaspar Joachim Utz died of a second and long-expected stroke, in his apartment at No. 5 Široká Street, overlooking the Old Jewish Cemetery in Prague.

Three days later, at 7.45 a.m., his friend Dr Václav Orlík was standing outside the Church of St Sigismund, awaiting the arrival of the hearse and clutching seven of the ten pink carnations he had hoped to afford at the florist's. He noted with approval the first signs of spring. In a garden across the street, jackdaws with twigs in their beaks were wheeling above the lindens, and now and then a minor avalanche would slide from the pantiled roof of a tenement.

While Orlík waited, he was approached by a man with a curtain of grey hair that fell below the collar of his raincoat.

'Do you play the organ?' the man asked in a catarrhal voice.

'I fear not,' said Orlík.

'Nor do I,' the man said, and shuffled off down a side-street.

At 7.57 a.m., the same man unbolted from inside the immense baroque doors of the Church. Without a nod to Orlík he then climbed into the organ loft and, seating himself amid its choir of giltwood and trumpeting angels, began to play a funeral march composed of the two sonorous chords he had learned the day before: from the organist who was too lazy to stir from bed at this hour and had found, in the janitor, a replacement.

At 8 a.m., the hearse – a Tatra 603 – drew up outside the steps: in order to divert the People's attention from retrograde Christian rituals, the authorities had decreed that all baptisms, weddings and funerals must be over by 8.30. Three of the pall-bearers got out, and helped each other open the rear door.

Utz had planned his own funeral with meticulous care. A blanket of white carnations covered the oak coffin – although he had not foreseen the wreath of Bolshevik vulgarity that had been placed on top: red poinsettias, red gladioli, red satin ribbon and a frieze of shiny laurel leaves. A card offered condolences (to whom?) from the Director of the Rudolfine Museum and his staff.

Orlík added his modest tribute.

A second Tatra brought the three remaining pall-bearers. They had squeezed themselves into the front seat beside the chauffeur while, on the back seat, sat a solitary woman in black, her black veil awash with tears. Since none of the men showed any inclination to help her, she pushed the door open and, shaking with grief, almost fell onto the slushy cobbles.

To relieve the pressure on her bunions the sides of her shoes were slit open.

Recognising her as Utz's faithful servant Marta, Orlík rushed to her assistance – and she, collapsing onto his shoulder, allowed him to escort her. When he attempted to carry her brown leatherette bag, she wrenched it from his grasp.

The bearers – employees of a rubber factory who worked night-shift and doubled for the undertaker by day – had shouldered the coffin and were advancing up the main aisle: to music that reminded Orlík of the tramp of soldiers on parade.

Halfway to the altar the procession met the cleaning woman, who, with soap, water and a scrubbing-brush, was scrubbing at the blazon of the Rožmberk family, inlaid into the floor in many-coloured marbles.

The leading bearer asked the woman, most politely,

to allow the coffin to pass. She scowled and went on scrubbing.

The bearers had no alternative but to take a left turn between two pews, a right turn up the side aisle, and another right to pass the pulpit. Eventually, they arrived before the altar where a youngish priest, his surplice stained with sacramental wine, was anxiously biting his fingernails.

They set down the coffin with a show of reverence. Then, attracted by the smell of hot bread from a bakery along the street, they strolled off to get breakfast leaving Orlík and the faithful Marta as the only mourners.

The priest mumbled the service at the speed of a patter number and, from time to time, lifted his eyes towards a fresco of the Heavenly Heights. After commending the dead man's soul, they had to wait at least ten minutes before the bearers condescended to return, at 8.26.

At the cemetery, from which the snow had almost melted, the priest, though wrapped in a thick serge overcoat, began to suffer from a fit of shivers. The coffin had hardly been lowered into the earth when he began to shove the moaning Marta, by the shoulder-blades, towards the waiting limousine. He declined Orlík's invitation to breakfast at the Hotel Bristol. At the corner of Jungmannova Street he shouted for the chauffeur to stop, and jumped out slamming the door.

It was Utz who had arranged, and paid for, this valedictory breakfast. An acrid smell of disinfectant flowed through the dining-room. Chairs were piled on tables, and more cleaning women were swabbing up the mess from a banquet held the previous evening, in honour of East German and Soviet computer experts. In the far left corner, a table covered in white damask was set for twenty people, with a fluted tokay glass at each place.

Utz had miscalculated. He had counted on at least a handful of his more venal cousins turning up, in case there was anything to be had. He had counted, too, on a delegation from the Museum: if only to arrange the transfer of his porcelains into their grasping hands.

As it was, Marta and Orlík sat alone, side by side, ordering smoked ham, cheese pancakes and wine from the slovenly waiter.

At the far end of the table stood a huge stuffed bear, reared on its hind-legs, mouth agape, forepaws outstretched – placed there by some humorous person to remind the clientele of their country's fraternal protector. On its plinth, a brass plaque announced that it had been shot by a Bohemian baron, not in the Tatras or Carpathians, but in the Yukon in 1926. The bear was a grizzly.

After a glass or two of tokay, Marta had apparently given up grieving for her dead employer. After four glasses, she twisted her mouth into a mocking grin and shouted at the top of her voice: 'To the Bear! . . . To the Bear!'

In the summer of 1967 – a year before the Soviet tanks overran Czechoslovakia – I went to Prague for a week of historical research. The editor of a magazine, knowing of my interest in the Northern Renaissance, had commissioned me to write an article on the Emperor Rudolf II's passion for collecting exotica: a passion which, in his later years, was his only cure for depression.

I intended the article to be part of a larger work on the psychology – or psychopathology – of the compulsive collector. As it turned out, due to idleness and my ignorance of the languages, this particular foray into Middle European studies came to nothing. I remember the episode as a very enjoyable holiday, at others' expense.

On my way to Czechoslovakia I had stopped at Schloss Ambras, outside Innsbruck, to see the Kunstkammer or 'cabinet of curiosities' assembled by Rudolf's uncle, Archduke Ferdinand of the Tyrol. (Uncle and nephew had a friendly but long-standing quarrel as to who should possess the Hapsburg family narwhal horn, and a Late Roman agate tazza that might or might not be the Holy Grail.)

The Ambras Collection, with its Cellini salt-cellar and Montezuma's headdress of quetzal plumes, had survived intact from the sixteenth to the nineteenth centuries when imperial officials, mindful of the revolutionary mob, removed its more spectacular treasures to Vienna. Rudolf's treasures – his mandragoras, his basilisk, his bezoar stone, his unicorn cup, his gold-mounted coco-de-mer, his homunculus in alcohol, his nails from Noah's Ark and the phial of dust from which God created Adam – had long ago vanished from Prague.

All the same, I wanted to see the gloomy palace-fortress, the Hradschin, where this secretive bachelor – who spoke Italian to his mistresses, Spanish to his God, German to his courtiers and Czech, seldom, to his rebellious peasants – would, for weeks on end, neglect the affairs of his Holy and Roman Empire and shut himself away with his astronomers (Tycho Brahé and Kepler were his protégés). Or search with his alchemists for the Philosopher's Stone. Or debate with learned rabbis the mysteries of the Cabbala. Or, as the crises of his reign intensified, imagine himself a hermit in the mountains. Or have his portrait done by Arcimboldo, who painted the Emperor's visage as a mound of fruit and vegetables, with a courgette and aubergine for the neck, and a radish for the Adam's apple.

Knowing no one in Prague, I asked a friend, a historian who specialised in the Iron Curtain countries, if there was anyone he'd recommend me to see.

He replied that Prague was still the most mysterious of European cities, where the supernatural was always a possibility. The Czechs' propensity to 'bend' before superior force was not necessarily a weakness. Rather, their metaphysical view of life encouraged them to look on acts of force as ephemera.

'Of course,' he said, 'I could send you to any number of intellectuals. Poets, painters, filmmakers.' Providing I could face an interminable whine about the role of the artist in a totalitarian state, or wished to go to a party that would end in a partouse.

I protested. Surely he was exaggerating?

'No,' he shook his head. 'I don't think so.'

He would be the last to denigrate a man who risked the labour camp for publishing a poem in a foreign journal. But, in his view, the true heroes of this impossible situation were people who wouldn't raise a murmur against the Party or State — yet who seemed to carry the sum of Western Civilisation in their heads.

'With their silence,' he said, 'they inflict a final insult on the State, by pretending it does not exist.'

Where else would one find, as he had, a tram-ticket salesman who was a scholar of the Elizabethan stage? Or a street-sweeper who had written a philosophical commentary on the Anaximander Fragment?

He finished by observing that Marx's vision of an age of infinite leisure had, in one sense, come true. The State, in its efforts to wipe out 'traces of individualism', offered limitless time for the intelligent individual to dream his private and heretical thoughts.

I said my motive for visiting Prague was perhaps

more frivolous than his – and I explained my interest in the Emperor Rudolf.

'In that case I'll send you to Utz,' he said. 'Utz is a Rudolf of our time.'

Utz was the owner of a spectacular collection of Meissen porcelain which, through his adroit manoeuvres, had survived the Second World War and the years of Stalinism in Czechoslovakia. By 1967 it numbered over a thousand pieces – all crammed into the tiny two-roomed flat on Široká Street.

The Utzes of Krondorf had been a family of minor Saxon landowners with farms in the Sudetenland, prosperous enough to maintain a town house in Dresden, insufficiently grand to figure on the Almanach de Gotha. Among their ancestors they could point to a Crusading Knight. But better-born Saxons would pronounce their name with an air of bewilderment, even of disgust: 'Utz? Utz? No. It is impossible. Who is this people?'

There were reasons for their scorn. In Grimm's Etymological Wordbook, 'utz' carries any number of negative connotations: 'drunk', 'dimwit', 'card-sharp', 'dealer in dud horses'. 'Heinzen, Kunzen, Utzen oder Butzen', in the dialect of Lower Swabia, is the equivalent of 'Any old Tom, Dick or Harry'.

Utz's father was killed on the Somme in 1916, not before he had redeemed the family honour by winning Germany's highest military decoration 'Pour le Mérite'. His widow, whom he had met at Marienbad in 1905 – and had married to the anguish of his parents – was the daughter of a Czech revivalist historian, and of a Jewish heiress whose fortune came from railway shares.

Kaspar was her only grandchild.

As a boy, he spent a month of each summer at Céske Krížove, a neo-mediaeval castle between Prague and Tábor where this wasted old woman, whose sallow skin refused to wrinkle or hair turn to grey, sat crippled with arthritis in a salon hung with crimson brocade and overvarnished paintings of the Virgin.

A convert to Catholicism, she surrounded herself with unctuous and genuflecting priests who would extol the purity of her faith in the hope of financial rewards. The banks of begonias and cinerarias in her conservatory protected her from a magnificent sweep of the Central Bohemian countryside.

Various neighbours were affronted that a woman of her race should affect the outward forms of aristocratic life: to the extent of peopling her staircase with suits of armour, and of keeping a bear in a walled-off section of the moat. Yet, even before Sarajevo, she had foreseen the rising tide of Socialism in Europe, and, twirling a terrestrial globe as another woman might recite the rosary, she would point a finger to the far-flung places in which she had diversified her investments: a copper-mine in Chile, cotton in Egypt, a cannery in Australia, gold in South Africa.

She rejoiced in the thought that her fortune would go on increasing after her death. *Theirs* would vanish: in war or revolution; on horses, women and the gaming-tables. In Kaspar, a dark-haired, introspective boy with none of his father's high complexion, she recognised the pallor of the ghetto – and adored him.

It was at Čéske Krížove that this precocious child, standing on tiptoe before a vitrine of antique porcelain, found himself bewitched by a figurine of Harlequin that had been modelled by the greatest of Meissen modellers, J. J. Kaendler.

The Harlequin sat on a tree trunk. His taut frame was sheathed in a costume of multi-coloured chevrons. In one hand he waved an oxidised silver tankard; in the other a floppy yellow hat. Over his face there was a leering orange mask.

'I want him,' said Kaspar.

The grandmother blanched. Her impulse was to give him everything he asked for. But this time she said, 'No! One day perhaps. Not now.'

Four years later, to console him for the death of his father, the Harlequin arrived in Dresden in a specially made leather box, in time for a dismal Christmas celebration. Kaspar pivoted the figurine in the flickering candlelight and ran his pudgy fingers, lovingly, over the glaze and brilliant enamels. He had found his vocation: he would devote his life to collecting – 'rescuing' as he came to call it – the porcelains of the Meissen factory.

He neglected his schoolroom studies, yet studied the history of porcelain manufacture, from its origins in China to its rediscovery in Saxony in the reign of Augustus the Strong. He bought new pieces. He sold off those which were inferior, or cracked. By the age of nineteen he had published in the journal *Nunc* a lively defence of the Rococo style in porcelain – an art of playful curves from an age when men adored women – against the slur of the pederast Winckelmann: 'Porcelain is almost always made into idiotic puppets.'

Utz spent hours in the museums of Dresden, scrutinising the ranks of Commedia dell' Arte figures that had come from the royal collections. Locked behind glass, they seemed to beckon him into their secret, Lilliputian world – and also to cry for their release. His second publication was entitled 'The Private Collector':

'An object in a museum case', he wrote, 'must suffer the de-natured existence of an animal in the zoo. In any museum the object dies – of suffocation and the public gaze – whereas private ownership confers on the owner the right and the need to touch. As a young child will reach out to handle the thing it names, so the passionate collector, his eye in harmony with his hand, restores to the object the life-giving touch of its maker. The collector's enemy is the museum curator. Ideally, museums should be looted every fifty years, and their collections returned to circulation . . . '

'What', Utz's mother asked the family physician, 'is this mania of Kaspar's for porcelain?'

'A perversion,' he answered. 'Same as any other.'

The sexual career of Augustus the Strong, as recounted by Von Pöllnitz in 'La Saxe Galant', served Utz as an exemplary model. But when, in a Viennese establishment, he aspired to imitate the conquests of that grandiose and insatiable monarch – hoping to discover in Mitzi, Suzi and Liesl the charms of an Aurora, Countess of Königsmark, a Mlle Kessel or any other goddess of the Dresden court – the girls were perplexed by the scientific seriousness of the young man's approach, and collapsed with giggles at the minuscule scale of his equipment.

He left, walking the wet streets alone to his hotel.

He got a warmer welcome from the antiquaires. The sale of his Sudetenland farms, in 1932, allowed him to spend money freely. The deaths, in quick succession, of his mother and grandmother, allowed him to bid against a Rothschild.

Politically, Utz was neutral. There was a timid side to his character that would tolerate any ideology providing it left him in peace. There was a stubborn side that refused to be bullied. He detested violence, yet welcomed the cataclysms that flung fresh works of art onto the market. 'Wars, pogroms and revolutions', he used to say, 'offer excellent opportunities for the collector.'

The Stock Market Crash had been one such opportunity. Kristallnacht was another. In the same week he hastened to Berlin to buy porcelains, in U.S. dollars, from Jewish connoisseurs who wished to emigrate. At the end of the War he would offer a similar service to aristocrats fleeing from the Soviet Army.

As a citizen of the Reich he accepted the annexation of the Sudetenland, albeit without enthusiasm. The occupation of Prague, however, made him realise that Hitler would soon unleash a European war. He also realised, on the principle that invaders invariably come to grief, that Germany would fail to win.

Acting on this insight, he succeeded in removing thirty-seven crates of porcelain from the family house in Dresden. These arrived at Céske Krížove during the summer of 1939. He did not unpack them.

About a year later, shortly after the Blitzkrieg, he had a visit from his red-headed second cousin, Reinhold: a clever but fundamentally silly character, who, as a student, had sworn that Kropotkin's 'Mutual Aid' was the greatest book ever written; who now expounded his views of racial biology with analogies culled from dog-breeding. An Utz, he insinuated, even if tainted with alien blood, should at once assume the uniform of the Wehrmacht.

At dinner, Utz listened politely while his cousin crowed over the victories in France: but when the man prophesied that Germans would occupy Buckingham Palace before the end of the year, he felt, despite his better judgement, a surge of latent anglophilia.

'I do not believe so,' he heard himself saying. 'You underestimate this people. I know them. I was in England myself.'

'*Also*,' the cousin murmured, and, with a click of

the heels, marched out towards his waiting staff-car.

Utz had indeed been to England, to learn English at the age of sixteen. During an autumn and dismal December, he had boarded at Bexhill-on-Sea with his mother's former nanny, Miss Beryl Parkinson, in a house of cats and cuckoo-clocks from which he would gaze at the turgid waves that broke across the pier.

He did learn some English – not much! He also made a short trip to London, and came away with a vivid notion of how an English gentleman behaved, and how he dressed. He returned to Dresden in a racily-cut tweed jacket, and a pair of hand-made brogues.

It was this same brown jacket, a little threadbare, a couple of sizes too small, and with leather patches sewn onto the elbows, that he would wear throughout the War – as an act of faith and defiance – whenever German officers were present.

He wore it, too, his racial purity called into question, during the reign of Reinhard Heydrich, 'The Butcher of Prague': one afternoon, he confounded his interrogators by pulling from its pocket his father's First War decoration. How dare they! he shouted, as he slapped the medal onto the table. How dare they insult the son of a great German soldier?

It was a bold stroke, and it worked. They gave him

no further trouble. He lay low at Céske Krížove and, for the first time in his life, took regular exercise: working with his foresters at the saw-mill. On February 16th 1945 news came that the Dresden house was flattened. His love of England vanished forever on hearing the B.B.C. announcer, 'There is no china in Dresden today.' He gave the jacket to a gipsy who had escaped the camps.

A month after the surrender, when Germans and German-supporters were being hounded from their homes – or escorted to the frontier 'in the clothes they stood up in' – Utz succeeded in disavowing his German passport and obtaining Czech nationality. He had a harder time dispelling rumours that he had helped in the activities of Goering's art squad.

The rumours were true. He had collaborated. He had given information: a trickle of information as to the whereabouts of certain works of art – information available to anyone who knew how to use an art library. By doing so, he had been able to protect, even to hide, a number of his Jewish friends: among them the celebrated Hebraist, Zikmund Kraus. What, after all, was the value of a Titian or a Tiepolo if one human life could be saved?

As for the Communists, once he realised the Beneš Government would fall, he began to curry favour with the bosses-to-be. On learning that Klement Gottwald had installed himself in Prague Castle, 'a worker on the throne of the Bohemian kings', Utz's reaction was to give his lands to a farming collective, and his own castle for use as an insane asylum.

These measures gave him time: sufficient at least to evacuate the porcelains, without loss or breakage, before they were requisitioned by the canaille.

His next move was to make a show of taking up Hebrew studies under the guidance of Dr Kraus: these were the years when pictures of Marx and Lenin used to hang in Israeli kibbutzes. He got a poorly paid job, as a cataloguer in the National Library. He installed himself in an inconspicuous flat in Židovské Město: its previous inhabitant having vanished in the Heydrichiada.

Twice a week he went loyally to watch a Soviet film.

When his friend Dr Orlík suggested they both flee to the West, Utz pointed to the ranks of Meissen figurines, six deep on the shelves, and said, 'I cannot leave them.'

'How did he get away with it?'
'With what?'

'The porcelain. How did he hang on to it?'

'He did a deal.'

My friend the historian gave me an outline of the facts as he knew them. It seems that the Communist authorities – ever ready to assume a veneer of legality – had allowed Utz to keep the collection providing every piece was photographed and numbered. It was also agreed – although never put in writing – that, after his death, the State Museums would get the lot.

Besides, Marxist-Leninism had never got to grips with the concept of the private collection. Trotsky, around the time of the Third International, had made a few offhand comments on the subject. But no one had ever decided if the ownership of a work of art damned its owner in the eyes of the Proletariat. Was the collector a class-enemy? If so, how?

The Revolution, of course, postulated the abolition of private property without ever defining the tenuous borderline between property (which was harmful to society) and household goods (which were not). A painting by a great master might rank as a national treasure, and be liable for confiscation – and there were families in Prague who kept their Picassos and Matisses rolled up between the floor joists. But porcelain? Porcelain could also be classed as crockery. So, providing it wasn't smuggled from the country, it was, in theory, valueless. To start confiscating ceramic statuettes could turn into an administrative nightmare:

'Imagine trying to confiscate an infinite quantity of plaster-of-Paris Lenins . . . '

His face was immediately forgettable. It was a round face, waxy in texture, without a hint of the passions beneath its surface, set with narrow eyes behind steel-framed spectacles: a face so featureless it gave the impression of not being there. Did he have a moustache? I forget. Add a moustache, subtract a moustache: nothing would alter his utterly nondescript appearance. Supposing, then, we add a moustache? A precise, bristly moustache to go with the precise, toy-soldierish gestures that were the only evidence of his Teuton ancestry? He had combed his hair in greasy snakes across his scalp. He wore a suit of striped grey worsted slightly frayed at the cuffs, and had doused himself with Knize Ten cologne.

On reflection, I think I'd better withdraw the moustache. To add a moustache might so overwhelm the face that nothing would linger in the memory but the spectacles and a moustache – with a few drops of paprika-coloured fish-soup adhering to it – across our table at the Restaurant Pstruh.

'Pstruh' is Czech for 'trout' – and trout there were! The cadences of the 'Trout' Quintet flowed methodically through hidden speakers and shoals of trout – pink, freckled, their undersides shimmering in the neon – swam this way and that way in an aquarium which occupied most of one wall.

'You will eat trout,' said Utz.

I had called him on the day of my arrival, but at first he seemed reluctant to see me:

'Ja! Ja! I know it. But it will be difficult . . . '

On the advice of my friend, I had brought from London some packets of his favourite Earl Grey tea. I mentioned these. He relented and asked me to luncheon: on the Thursday, the day before I was due to leave – not, as I had hoped, at his flat, but in a restaurant.

The restaurant, a relic of the Thirties in an arcade

off Wenceslas Square, had a machine-age décor of plate-glass, chromium and leather. A model galleon, with sails of billowing parchment, hung from the ceiling. One wondered, glancing at the photo of Comrade Novotný, how a man with so disagreeable a mouth would consent to being photographed at all. The head-waiter, sweltering in the July heat, offered each of us a menu that resembled a mediaeval missal.

We were expecting the arrival of Utz's friend, Dr Orlík, with whom he had lunched here on Thursdays since 1946.

'Orlík', he told me, 'is an illustrious scientist from our National Museum. He is a palaeontologue. His speciality is the mammoth, but he is also experienced in flies. You will enjoy him. He is full of jokes and charm.'

We did not have long to wait before a gaunt, bearded figure in a shiny double-breasted suit pushed its way through the revolving doors. Orlík removed his beret, revealing a mass of wiry salt-and-pepper hair, and sat down. His hand – rather a crustacean claw than a hand – gave mine a painful nip and moved on to attack the pretzels. His forehead was scoured with deep furrows. I stared with amazement at the see-saw motion of his jaw.

'Ah! Ha!' he leered at me. 'English, he? Englishman! Yes. YES! Tell me, is Professor Horsefield still living?'

'Who's Horsefield?' I asked.

'He wrote kind words about my article in the "Journal of Animal Psychology".'

'When was that?'

'1935,' he said. 'Maybe '36.'

'I've never heard of Horsefield.'

'A pity,' said Orlík. 'He was an illustrious scientist.'

He paused to crunch the remaining pretzel. His green eyes glinted with playful malice.

'Normally,' he continued, 'I do not have high regard for your compatriots. You betrayed us at München . . . You betrayed us at Yalta . . . '

Utz, alarmed by this dangerous turn to the conversation, interrupted and said, solemnly, 'I cannot believe that animals have souls.'

'How can you say that?' Orlík snapped.

'I say it.'

'I know you say it. I know not how you can say it.'

'I will order,' said Utz, who waved his napkin, like a flag of truce, at the head-waiter. 'I will order trout. "Au bleu", isn't it?'

'Blau,' Orlík bantered.

'Blau yourself.'

Orlík tugged at my sleeve: 'My friend Mr Utz here believes that the trout, when it is immersed in boiling water, does not feel more than a tickling. That is not my opinion.'

'There are no trout,' said the head-waiter.

'What can you mean, no trout?' said Utz. 'There are trout. *Many* trout.'

'There is no net.'

'What can you mean, no net? Last week there was a net.'

'Is broken.'

'Broken, I do not believe.'

The head-waiter put a finger to his lips, and whispered, 'These trout are reserved.'

'For them?'

'Them,' he nodded.

Four fat men were eating trout at a nearby table.

'Very well,' said Utz. 'I will eat eels. You also will eat eels?'

'I will,' I said.

'There are no eels,' said the waiter.

'No eels? This is bad. What have you?'

'We have carp.'

'Carp only?'

'Carp.'

'How shall you cook this carp?'

'Many ways,' the waiter gestured to the menu. 'Which way you like.'

The menu was multilingual: in Czech, Russian, German, French and English. But whoever had compiled the English page had mistaken the word 'carp' for 'crap'. Under the heading CRAP DISHES, the list contained 'Crap soup with paprika', 'Stuffed crap', 'Crap cooked in beer', 'Fried crap', 'Crap balls', 'Crap à la juive . . . '

'In England,' I said, 'this fish is called "carp". "Crap" has a different meaning.'

'Oh?' said Dr Orlík. 'What meaning?'

'Faeces,' I said. 'Shit.'

I regretted saying this because Utz looked exceedingly embarrassed. The narrow eyes blinked, as if he hoped he hadn't heard correctly. Orlík's wheezy carapace shook with laughter.

'Ha! Ha!' he jeered. 'Crap à la juive . . . My friend Mr Utz will eat Crap à la juive . . . !'

I was afraid Utz was going to leave, but he rose above his discomfiture and ordered soup and the 'Carpe meunière'. I took the line of least resistance and ordered the same. Orlík clamoured in his loud and crackly voice, 'No. No. I will eat "Crap à la juive" . . . !'

'And to begin?' asked the waiter.

'Nothing,' said Orlík. 'Only the crap!'

I tried to swing the conversation to Utz's collection of porcelain. His reaction was to swivel his neck inside his collar and say, blankly, 'Dr Orlík is also a collector. But he is a collector of flies.'

'Flies?'

'Flies,' assented Orlík.

I began to form a mental picture of his lodgings: the unmade bed and unemptied ash-trays; the avalanche of yellowing periodicals; the microscope; the killing-jars and, lining the walls, glass-fronted cases containing flies from every corner of the globe, each specimen pierced with a pin. I mentioned some beautiful dragonflies I had seen in Brazil.

'Dragonflies?' Orlík frowned. 'I have not interest. I have only interest for Musca domestica.'

'The common house-fly?'

'That is what it is.'

'Answer me,' Utz interrupted again. 'On which day did God create the fly? Day Five? Or Day Six?'

'How many times will I tell you?' Orlík clamoured. 'We have one hundred ninety million years of flies. But you will always speak of days!'

'Hard words,' said Utz, philosophically.

A fly had landed on the tablecloth and was sopping up some soup that the waiter had let fall from the ladle. With a flick of the wrist Orlík upturned a glass tumbler, and trapped the insect beneath it. He slid the glass to the edge of the table and transferred the fly to the killing-jar he took from his pocket. There was an angry buzzing, then silence.

He flourished a magnifying glass and scrutinised the victim.

'Interesting example,' he said. 'Hatched, I would say, in the kitchen here. I will ask . . . '

'You will not ask,' said Utz.

'I will. I will ask.'

'You will not.'

'And what', I asked, 'brought you and the house-fly together?'

Expelling carp bones through his beard, Orlík described how he had devoted thirty years to studying certain aspects of the woolly mammoth: a labour which had taken him to the tundras of Siberia where mammoths are occasionally found deep-frozen in permafrost. The fruit of these researches – though he was usually too modest to mention it – had culminated in his magisterial paper 'The Mammoth and His Parasites'. But no sooner was it published than he felt the need to study some lowlier creature.

'I chose', he said, 'to study Musca domestica within the Prague Metropolitan area.'

Just as his friend Mr Utz could tell at a glance whether a piece of Meissen porcelain was made from the white clay of Colditz or the white clay of Erzgebirge, he, Orlík, having examined under a microscope the iridescent membrane of a fly's wing, claimed to know if the insect came from Malá Strana or Židovské Město or from one of the garbage dumps that now encircled the New Garden City.

He confessed to being enchanted by the vitality of the fly. It was fashionable among his fellow entomologists – especially the Party Members – to applaud the behaviour of the social insects: the ants, bees, wasps and other varieties of Hymenoptera which organised themselves into regimented communities.

'But the fly', said Orlík, 'is an anarchist.'

'Sssh!' said Utz. 'You will not say that word!'

'What word?'

'That word.'

'Yes. Yes,' Orlík pitched his voice an octave higher. 'I will say it. The fly is an anarchist. He is an individualist. He is a Don Juan.'

The four fat Party Members, at whom this outburst was directed, were far too busy to notice: they were ogling their second helping of trout whose flesh, at that moment, the waiter was easing off the bone and blue skin.

'I am not from the People,' Orlík said. 'I have noble blood.'

'Oh?' said Utz. 'Which nobility?'

I thought for a moment that lunch was going to end in a slanging match – until I realised that this was another of their well-rehearsed duets. There followed a discussion on the merits (or otherwise) of Kafka, whom Utz revered as a demiurge and Orlík dismissed as a fraud. It was right for his books to be abolished.

'Banned, you mean?' I said. 'Censored?'

'I do not mean,' said Orlík. 'I said abolished.'

'Paf! Paf!' Utz flapped his hand. 'What foolishness is this?'

Orlík's case against Kafka was the doubtful entomological status of the insect in the story 'Metamorphosis'. Again, I thought we were in for trouble. Again, the brouhaha simmered down. We drank a cup of anaemic coffee. Orlík extracted from me my London address, scribbled it on a scrap of paper napkin, rolled it into a pellet, and put it in his pocket.

He intercepted the bill and waved it in Utz's face.

'I will pay,' he announced.

'You will not pay.'

'I will. I must.'

'You will not,' said Utz, who snatched at the paper Orlík held for him to snatch.

Orlík's eyelids dropped in acquiescence.

'Aah!' he nodded gloomily. 'I know it. Mr Utz will pay.'

'And now,' Utz turned to me, 'you will permit me to show you some monuments of our beautiful city.'

Utz and I spent the rest of the afternoon strolling through the thinly peopled streets of Malá Strana, pausing now and then to admire the blistering façade of a merchant's house, or some Baroque or Rococo palace – the Vrtba, the Pálffy, the Lobkovic: he recited their names as though the builders were intimate friends.

In the Church of Our Lady Victorious, the waxen Spanish image of the Christ Child, aureoled in an explosion of gold, seemed less the Blessed Babe of Bethlehem than the vengeful divinity of the Counter-Reformation.

We climbed the length of Neruda Street and walked around the Hradschin: the scene of my futile researches during the previous week. We then sat in an orchard below the Strahov Monastery. A man in his underpants sunned himself on the grass. The fluff of balsam poplars floated by, and settled on our clothes like snowflakes.

'You will see,' said Utz, waving his malacca over the multiplicity of porticoes and cupolas below us. 'This city wears a tragic mask.'

It was also a city of giants: giants in stone, in stucco or marble; naked giants; blackamoor giants; giants dressed as if for a hurricane, not one of them in repose, struggling with some unseen force, or heaving under the weight of architraves.

'The suffering giant', he added without conviction, 'is the emblem of our persecuted people.'

I commented facetiously that a taste for giants was usually a symptom of decline: an age that took the Farnese Hercules for an ideal was bound to end in trouble.

Utz countered with the story of Frederick William of Prussia who had once made a collection of real giants – semi-morons mostly – to swell the ranks of his Potsdam Grenadiers.

He then explained how this weakness for giants had led to one of the most bizarre diplomatic transactions of the eighteenth century: in which Augustus of Saxony chose 127 pieces of Chinese porcelain from the Palace of Charlottenburg, in Berlin, and gave in return 600 giants 'of the required height' collected in the eastern provinces.

'I never liked giants,' he said.

'I once met a man,' I said, 'who was a dealer in dwarfs.'

'Oh?' he blinked. 'Dwarfs, you say?'

'Dwarfs.'

'Where did you meet this man?'

'On a plane to Baghdad. He was going to view a dwarf for a client.'

'A client! This is wonderful!'

'He had two clients,' I said. 'One was an Arab oil sheikh. The other owned hotels in Pakistan.'

'And what did they do with those dwarfs?' Utz tapped me on the knee.

He had paled with excitement and was mopping the sweat from his brow.

'Kept them,' I said. 'The sheikh, if I remember right, liked to sit his favourite dwarf on his forearm and his favourite falcon on the dwarf's forearm.'

'Nothing else?'

'How can one know?'

'You are right,' said Utz. 'These are things one cannot know.'

'Or would want to.'

'And what would cost a dwarf? These days?'

'Who can say? Collecting dwarfs has always been expensive.'

'That's a nice story,' he smiled at me. 'Thank you. I also like dwarfs. But not in the way you think.'

It was now early evening and we were sitting on a slatted seat in the Old Jewish Cemetery. Pigeons were burbling on the roof of the Klausen Synagogue. The sunbeams, falling through sycamores, lit up spirals of midges and landed on the mossy tombstones, which, heaped one upon the other, resembled seaweed-covered rocks at low-tide.

To our right, a party of American Hasids – pale, short-sighted youths in yarmulkes – were laying pebbles on the tomb of the Great Rabbi Loew. They posed for a photograph, with their backs to its scrolling headstone.

Utz told me how the original ghetto – that warren of secret passages and forgotten rooms so vividly described by Meyrink – had been replaced by apartment buildings after the slum clearances of the 1890s. The synagogues, the cemetery and the Old Town Hall were almost the only monuments to survive. These, he said, far from being destroyed by the Nazis, were spared to form a proposed Museum of Jewry, where Aryan tourists of the future would inspect the relics of a people as lost as the Aztecs or Hottentots.

He changed the subject.

'You have heard tell the story of the Golem?'

'I have,' I said. 'The Golem was an artificial man . . . a mechanical man . . . a prototype of the robot. He was a creation of the Rabbi Loew.'

'My friend,' he smiled, 'you know, I think, many things. But you have many things to know.'

The Rabbi Loew had been the undisputed leader of Prague Jewry in the reign of the Emperor Rudolf: never again would the Jews of Middle Europe enjoy such esteem and privilege. He entertained princes and ambassadors, and was entertained by his sovereign in the Hradschin. Many of his writings – among them the homily 'On the Hardening of Pharaoh's Heart' – were absorbed into the teachings of Hasidism. Like any other Cabbalist he believed that every event – past, present and future – was already written down in the Torah.

After his death, the Rabbi was inevitably credited with supernatural powers. There are tales – none dating from his lifetime – of how, with an abracadabra, he moved a castle from the Bohemian countryside to the Prague ghetto. Or told the Emperor to his face that his real father was a Jew. Or trounced the mad Jesuit, Father Thaddeus, and proved the Jews were innocent of blood guilt. Or fashioned Yossel the Golem from the glutinous mud of the River Vltava.

All golem legends derived from an Ancient Jewish belief that any righteous man could create the World by repeating, in an order prescribed by the Cabbala, the letters of the secret name of God. 'Golem' meant 'unformed' or 'uncreated' in Hebrew. Father Adam himself had been 'golem' – an inert mass of clay so vast as to cover the ends of the Earth: that is, until Yahweh shrank him to human scale and breathed into his mouth the power of speech.

'So you see,' said Utz, 'not only was Adam the first human person. He was also the first ceramic sculpture.'

'Are you suggesting your porcelains are alive?'

'I am and I am not,' he said. 'They are alive and they are dead. But if they *were* alive, they would also have to die. Is it not?'

'If you say so.'

'Good. So I say it.'

'Good,' I said. 'Go on about golems.'

One of Utz's favourite golem stories was a mediaeval text discovered by Gershom Scholem: wherein it was written that Jesus Christ ('like *our* friend J. J. Kaendler') used to make model birds from clay – which, once He had uttered the sacred formula, would sing, flap their wings and fly.

A second story ('Oh! What a Jewish story!') told of two hungry rabbis who, having fashioned the figure of a calf, brought it to life – then cut its throat and ate veal for supper.

As for making a golem, a recipe in the Sepher Yetzirah or 'Book of Creation' called for a quantity of untouched mountain soil. This was to be kneaded with fresh spring water and, from it, a human image formed. The maker was required to recite over each of the image's limbs the appropriate alphabetical combination. He then walked around it clockwise a number of times: whereupon the golem stood and lived. Were he to reverse the direction, the creature would revert to clay.

None of the earlier sources say whether or not a golem could speak. But the automaton did have the gift of memory and would obey orders mechanically, without reflection, providing these were given at regular intervals. If not, the golem might run amok.

Golems also gained in stature, inch by inch, every day: yearning, it would seem, to attain the gigantic size of the Cosmic Adam — and so crush their creators and overwhelm the world.

'There was no end', said Utz, 'to the size of golems. Golems were highly dangerous.'

A golem was said to wear a slip of metal known as the 'shem', either across its forehead or under its tongue. The 'shem' was inscribed with the Hebrew word 'emeth', or Truth of God. When a rabbi wished to destroy his golem, he had only to pluck out the opening letter, so that 'emeth' now read 'meth' — which is to say 'death' — and the golem dissolved.

'I see,' I said. 'The "shem" was a kind of battery?'

'It was.'

'Without which the machine wouldn't work?'

'Also.'

'And the Rabbi Loew . . . ?'

'Wanted a servant. He was a good Jewish business-man. He wanted a servant without paying wages.'

'And a servant that wouldn't answer back!'

Yossel was the name of the Rabbi Loew's golem. On weekdays he did all sorts of menial tasks. He chopped wood, swept the street and the synagogue, and acted as watchdog in case the Jesuits got up to mischief. Yet on the Sabbath – since all God's creatures must rest on the Sabbath – his master would remove the 'shem' and render him lifeless for a day.

One Sabbath the Rabbi forgot to do this, and Yossel went berserk. He pulled down houses, threw rocks, threatened people and tore up trees by the roots. The congregation had already filled the Altneu Synagogue for morning prayers, and was chanting the 92nd Psalm: 'My horn shalt thou exalt like the horn of the unicorn . . . ' The Rabbi rushed into the street and snatched the 'shem' from the monster's forehead.

Another version places the 'death', amid old books and prayer-shawls, in the loft of the synagogue.

'Tell me,' I asked, 'would a golem have had Jewish features?'

'Not!' Utz answered with a touch of impatience. 'The golem was always a servant. Servants in Jewish houses were always of the goyim.'

45

'Would a golem have had Nordic features?'

'Yes,' he agreed. 'Giants' features.'

Utz brooded for a while and then arrived at the crux of the discussion:

All these tales suggested that the golem-maker had acquired arcane secrets: yet, in doing so, had transgressed Holy Law. A man-made figure was a blasphemy. A golem, by its presence alone, issued a warning against idolatry – and actively beseeched its own destruction.

'Would you say then', I asked, 'that art-collecting is idolatry?'

'Ja! Ja!' he struck his chest. 'Of course! Of course! That is why we Jews . . . and in this matter I consider myself a Jew . . . are so *good* at it! Because it is forbidden . . . ! Because it is sinful . . . ! Because it is dangerous . . . !'

'Do your porcelains demand their own death?'

He stroked his chin.

'I do not know. It is a very problematical question.'

The other visitors had left. A black cat had positioned itself on the crest of a tombstone. The guardian told us it was time to leave.

'And now my friend,' said Utz, 'would it amuse you to see my collection of dwarfs?'

An odour of suppurating cabbage leaves seeped from a dustbin in the entrance hall. A rat hopped off as we approached. In an apartment on the second landing, a baby wailed and someone was trying to master one of Dvořák's 'Slavonic Dances' on an out-of-tune piano. On the third landing a woman opened her door to see who was passing: a hysterical face under a heap of auburn curls. She wore a peignoir of magenta peonies, and vehemently slammed the door shut.

'She is mad,' Utz apologised. 'She was a famous soprano.'

On the top floor, he caught his breath, fumbled for his latch-key and ushered me inside. The smell was familiar to me: the stale smell of rooms where works of art are kept, and dusting considered dangerous. In a dingy green kitchenette off the hallway, Utz's servant sat perched on a stool.

She was a solid woman dressed awkwardly in a maid's uniform, with glowing cheeks and sandy hair flecked with grey. Over a black woollen dress there was a frilly white apron and, across her forehead, a fillet of lace. Her legs were encased in black stockings, which had a pair of white 'potatoes' at the knee.

She was expecting us.

In her lap she cradled a dish of emblazoned white porcelain which, I knew from my 'arty' days, was a piece of the celebrated Swan Service made by Kaendler for the Saxon First Minister, Count Brühl. On it she had arranged some slivers of cheese and crackers, Hungarian salami and rounds of pickled cucumber cut in the form of flowers.

She bowed her head deferentially.

'Guten Abend, Herr Baron.'

'Guten Abend, Marta,' he returned her greeting.

We moved into the room. Behind the net curtain, a single north-facing window looked out over the trees of the cemetery.

'I didn't know you were a baron,' I said.

'Yes,' he blushed. 'I am a baron also.'

The room, to my surprise, was decorated in the 'modern style': almost devoid of furniture apart from a daybed, a glass-topped table and a pair of Barcelona chairs upholstered in dark green leather. Utz had 'rescued' these in Moravia, from a house built by Mies van der Rohe.

It was a narrow room, made narrower by the double bank of plate-glass shelves, all of them crammed with porcelain, that reached from floor to ceiling. The shelves were backed with mirror, so that you had the illusion of entering an enfilade of glittering chambers, a 'dream palace' multiplied to infinity, through which human forms flitted like insubstantial shadows.

The carpet was grey. You had to watch your step for fear of tripping over one of the white porcelain sculptures – a pelican, a turkey-cock, a bear, a lynx and a rhino – modelled either by Kaendler or Eberlein for the Japanese Palace in Dresden. All five were scarred with fissures caused by faults in the firing.

Utz waved to some bottles on the table: scotch, slivovic, and a soda siphon.

'It is scotch, isn't it?'

'Scotch,' I said.

At the whoosh of the siphon, the maid emerged with her canapés on the Swan Service dish. Her movements seemed so lifeless and mechanical you would have thought that Utz had created a female golem. Yet I detected the suggestion of a superior smile.

'Cheerio!' said Utz, mimicking an English gentleman's accent.

'Your health!' I raised my glass – and took stock of my surroundings.

I am not an expert on Meissen porcelain – although my years of traipsing round art museums have taught me what it is. Nor can I say I like Meissen porcelain. I do, however, admire the boisterous energy of an artist such as Kaendler, at play with a medium which was totally new. And I entirely side with Utz in his feud with Winckelmann – who, in his 'Notes on the Plebeian Taste in Porcelain', would supplant this plebeian vitality with the dead hand of classical perfection.

I am equally fascinated by the way in which 'porcelain sickness' – the Porzellankrankheit of Augustus the Strong – so warped his vision, and that of his ministers, that their delirious schemes for ceramics got confused with real political power. Of Brühl, who would become Director of the Meissen Manufactory, Horace Walpole commented tartly: ' . . . he had prepared nothing but bawbles against a prince (Frederick the Great) that lived in a camp with the frugality of a common soldier . . . '

Utz had chosen each item to reflect the moods and facets of the 'Porcelain Century': the wit, the charm, the gallantry, the love of the exotic, the heartlessness and light-hearted gaiety – before they were swept away by revolution and the tramp of armies.

Arranged along the longer set of shelves were plates, vases, flagons and tureens. There were tea-caddies of polished redware by the 'inventor' of porcelain, Johannes Böttger. There were Böttger tankards with silver-gilt mounts; teapots with 'Watteau' scenes; teapots with eagle-headed spouts and teapots painted with goldfish, after Chinese and Japanese models.

Utz came up behind me, breathing heavily.

'Beautiful, no?'

'Beautiful,' I repeated.

He showed me an excellent example of 'indianische Blumen', and a turquoise bowl painted by Horoldt, with a panel of Augustus enthroned as The Emperor of China.

He showed me the Meissen imitations of K'ang Hsi blue-and-white: the porcelain his hero Augustus had loved so passionately; for which he had emptied his treasury to the dealers of Paris and Amsterdam, causing his Minister of Industry, Graf von Tschirnhaus, to moan, 'China is the bleeding-bowl of Saxony'.

Pride of place, however, was given to a Swan Service tureen: a Rococo fantasy on legs of intertwined fishes, the handles in the form of nereids, the lid heaped high with flowers, shells, swans and a bug-eyed dolphin – which, but for the bravura of its execution, would have been a monstrosity.

I gasped: knowing that the way to endear oneself to an art-collector is to rhapsodise his things.

'Come,' he beckoned me across the room.

I picked my way around the pelican and the rhino and arrived at the second bank of shelves where, in rows of five and six, were assembled a multitude of eighteenth-century figurines, all dazzlingly clothed and coloured.

I saw the characters of the Commedia dell' Arte: Harlequin and Columbine, Brighella and Pantaloon, Scaramouche and Truffaldino; The Doctor with a corkscrew for a beard; The Captain, who, being Spanish, had a jet-black moustache.

Utz reminded me how the Italian players – the real ones! – had been masters of extempore who would decide what to play, and how to play it, a mere five minutes before the curtain rose.

He pointed to the Personification of the Continents: Africa in leopard skin, America in feathers, Asia in a pagoda hat – while a lascivious, broad-bottomed Europa sat astride a white horse.

Next came the ladies of the Court: ladies with frozen smiles and swaying crinolines; their wigs were powdered, their cheeks pocked with beauty spots, and there were black bows tied around their necks. One lady caressed a pug. One kissed a Polish nobleman. Another kissed a Saxon while Harlequin peeped up her skirt. Madame de Pompadour, in a lilac dress scattered with roses, sang the aria from Lully's 'Acis and Galatea' which she had sung in real life, with the Prince de Rohan for a partner, in the Petit Théâtre de Versailles.

The lower orders were represented, each according to his or her occupation: the miner, the rope-maker, the woodcutter, the seamstress, the hairdresser and a fisherman, hopelessly drunk.

Shepherds trilled at their flutes. A Turk puffed a hookah. There were Tartars, Malabars, Circassians and Chinese sages with wispy beards and songbirds perched on their fingers. A party of freemasons scrutinised a globe. A pilgrim bore his staff and scallop-shell, and an endlessly grieving Mater Dolorosa sat next to a disconsolate nun.

'Bravo!' I cried. 'Unbelievable!'

'Now look at these funny fellows!' Utz was stroking the cheek of a grotesque buffoon. 'This one is Court Jester Fröhlich. That one is Postmaster Schmeidl.'

The two clowns used to perform at royal banquets, and keep everyone in stitches all night. Utz thought them as funny in porcelain as they were supposed to have been in real life. Schmeidl, he said, was terrified of mice.

This was why he chose to portray the Court Jester in the act of teasing his friend with a mouse-trap.

'Kaendler', he sniggered, 'was a witty man! A satirical man! He was always choosing persons to laugh at.'

I forced a nervous laugh.

'Now, Sir, if you please, look at this one!'

The model in question showed the soprano, Faustina Bordone, singing in ecstasy while a fox sat playing a spinet. Faustina, he said, had been the 'Callas of her day' and wife of the court composer, Hasse. She also had a lover called Fuchs.

'Fuchs,' said Utz, 'you must know in German means "fox".'

'I do know.'

'That is very amusing? No?'

'Very,' I laughed.

'Good. We agree on that one.'

He let fly an unexpectedly loud cackle, and went on shaking with laughter until Marta returned with her canapés and, with another 'Herr Baron!', silenced him.

The moment her back was turned he re-entered his world of little figures. His face lit up. He grinned, displaying a set of unhealthy pink gums, and showed me his monkey musicians.

'Lovely ones, aren't they?'

'Lovely,' I assented.

The monkeys wore ruffs and powdered wigs and, under the baton of a tyrannical conductor in a blue swallow-tailed coat, were fiddling and scraping, trumpeting, strumming and singing: in mockery of Count Brühl's private orchestra.

'I', Utz boasted, 'am the only private collector to possess the whole set.'

'Good for you!' I said, encouragingly.

Finally, we passed from the monkeys to the rest of the menagerie where there were wagtails, partridges, a bittern, a pair of sparrow-hawks, parrots and parakeets, orioles and roller birds, and peacocks displaying their tail feathers.

I counted a camel, a chamois, an elephant, a crocodile and a Lipizzaner led by a negro. Count Brühl's favourite pug-dog sat curled on a rose-velvet cushion while, on the bottom shelf, like a large albino fish, lay the life-size horse's tail in white porcelain intended — or so Utz said — for an equestrian statue of Augustus to be erected at the Judenhof in Dresden.

He then removed one of his seven figures of Harlequin — *the* Harlequin his grandmother gave him as a boy — and, turning it upside down, pointed to the 'cross-swords' mark of Meissen, and to an inventory label with a number and letters in code.

This was the label that earmarked the piece for the Museum.

'But those persons', Utz whispered, 'have made a mistake.'

One morning in February of 1952, a rap on the door demanded entry for three unwelcome visitors. They were a curator from the Museum; a photographer and an acne-pitted lout who, as Utz guessed, was a member of the secret police.

For the next two weeks he was a helpless witness while this trio turned the apartment upside down, trampled slush into the carpet, and made an inventory of every object. The curator warned him not to tamper with the labels. If he did so, the collection would be forfeit.

Utz particularly loathed the photographer: a grim, fanatical young woman with an astigmatism, who had worked herself into a fever of indignation. In her view, he had no business keeping treasures that rightfully belonged to the People.

'Really?' he answered. 'By what right? The right of theft, I suppose?'

The policeman told him to hold his tongue – or it would be worse for him.

The photographer converted the room into a makeshift studio, fussing over her plate-camera as though it were a thing beyond price. When Utz accidentally brushed against the lens, she ordered him into the bedroom.

She may have been a competent photographer: but she was so short-sighted, and so clumsy when handling the porcelains that Utz had to sit on the edge of his bed, numbly waiting for the crash. He begged to be allowed to position each piece in front of the camera. He was told it was none of his business.

Finally, when the young woman dropped, and smashed the head off, a figure of Watteau's Gilles, he lost his temper.

'Take it!' he snapped. 'Take it for your horrible museum! I never want to see it again.'

The photographer shrugged. The policeman wobbled his jowls. The curator went into the bathroom and, returning with a length of lavatory paper, wrapped the head and the torso separately, and put them in his pocket.

'This piece', he said, 'will not appear in the inventory.'

'Thank you,' said Utz. 'Thank you for that!'

At last, when they had gone, he gazed miserably at his miniature family. He felt abused and assaulted. He felt like the man who, on returning from a journey, finds his house has been burgled. He summoned up a few vague thoughts of suicide. There wasn't much — was there? — to live for. But no! He wasn't the type. He would never work up the courage. But could he bring himself to leave the collection? Make a clean break? Begin a new life abroad? He still had money in Switzerland, thank God! Who could tell? In Paris or in New York, he might even begin to collect again.

He decided, if he could get out, to go.

During the Gottwald years, the most reliable method of obtaining an exit visa was to apply for foreign travel on the grounds of ill-health. The procedure was to go to your usual physician, and ask him to diagnose an ailment.

'Do you suffer from depression?' Dr Petrasels demanded.

'Constantly,' said Utz. 'I always have.'

'Doubtless a malfunctioning of the liver,' said the doctor, who made no effort to examine him further. 'I advise you to take the cure at Vichy.'

'But surely . . . ?' Utz protested. Czechoslovakia was the land of spas. Surely they'd be suspicious? Surely there were waters for the liver at Marienbad? Or at Carlsbad?

'Far from it,' the doctor assured him. The visa authorities knew all about the waters of Vichy. Vichy was the place for him.

'If you say so,' said Utz, with misgivings.

The official in the visa department glanced at the medical report; mumbled the word 'Vichy' in a disinterested tone, and went to consult the file. A week later, when he returned to the same office, Utz learned he had been given a month's stay abroad. He undertook not to spread malicious propaganda against the People's Republic. The porcelain collection would be considered surety for his good behaviour, and his safe return.

The man insinuated that they had 'ways and means' of finding out where he went in Western Europe, and if he actually turned up at Vichy. Utz was astonished that no one bothered to ask how he would support himself in a foreign country. Was this, he wondered, a trap?

'What can they expect of me?' he asked himself. 'Subsist on air?'

O n the eve of his departure, his tickets and passport in order, he took leave of the collection piece by piece. Marta was cooking in the kitchenette. He had ordered dinner for two.

She had spread a fresh damask cloth over the glass-topped table; and as he surveyed the sparkling Swan Service plates, the salt-cellar, the cutlery with chinoiserie handles — he came close to believing in his fantasy: that this *was* the 'porcelain palace', and that he himself was Augustus reincarnate.

Marta, whom he had taught to make a soufflé, asked what time the guest would arrive. He stood up. He straightened his tie. Then, without a hint of condescension, he pressed her calloused hand to his lips.

'This evening, my dear Marta, you are to be the guest.'

She coloured at the neck. She protested. She said she was unworthy, and in the end accepted with delight.

Marta was the child of a village carpenter who lived near Kostelec in Southern Bohemia. His wife's early death, from tuberculosis, drove him to drink, and in a tavern brawl he almost killed a man. Ostracised, accused of the evil eye, he sent his two elder daughters to live with an aunt, and took the youngest along on his travels. He found work as a woodcutter on Utz's estate at Čéske Krížove. When he also died, crushed by a falling tree, the bailiff evicted the girl from their cottage.

She earned a few pennies doing chores for the baker or laundrywoman. Later, to avoid being sent to a workhouse, she went to live on a farm, where she slept on a straw-filled pallet and looked after a flock of geese.

She sang strange, incoherent songs and was thought to be simple: especially when she fell in love with a gander. Children in peasant Europe believed the tales they were told: of werewolves, of stars that were ducks in flight, or the gander who turned into a shining prince.

Marta's gander was a magnificent snow-white bird: the object of terror to foxes, children and dogs. She had reared him as a gosling; and whenever she approached, he would let fly a low contented burble and sidle his neck around her thighs. Some mornings, at first light when no one was about, she would swim with her lover in the lake, and allow him to nibble her long fair hair.

One morning, sometime in the late Thirties, as Utz was driving his Steyr coupé from the castle to catch the early train to Prague, he caught sight of a girl in dripping clothes being hounded down the street by a mob of villagers. He braked the car, and asked her to sit beside him.

'Come with me,' he said kindly.

She cringed, but obeyed. He drove her back to the castle.

A new life opened up for her, in domestic service. She followed her master's movements with an adoring gaze: frequently he had to prevent her from kissing his hand. Four years later, when he had put her in charge of the household, his other retainers, puzzled by the habits of this solitary bachelor, spread rumours that she shared his bed.

The truth was that, in a world of shifting allegiances – and since the death of his grandmother's faithful major-domo – she was the only person he could trust, and, at the same time, use. Only she knew the hay-loft where the Hebrew scholar Dr Kraus – and his Talmuds – was in hiding: she would risk her life to fetch him food. Only she had the key to the cellar where, throughout the War, the porcelains were stored.

Later, in the months after the Communist takeover, when the peasants, still bemused by propaganda, believed that the new ideology allowed them to divide the landlord's property, it was she who stood guard against them. Utz was free to leave the castle with his treasures.

In Prague, she slept in a leaky attic room a few doors down Široká Street. When interrogated about the terms of her employment, she bridled. She was not Mr Utz's employee. She looked after him merely as a friend.

He, by inviting her to share his table, affirmed that the friendship was shared.

Over dinner, he explained the reason for his journey. She dropped her knife and fork, and gasped, 'You're not ill, I hope.'

He calmed her fears, but gave no hint that he might never come back. She should sleep, meanwhile, in the apartment — in his bed if she wished it — and keep the door firmly locked. His friend, Dr Orlík, would look in from time to time, in case there was anything she needed.

The wine went to her head. She became a little flushed. She talked a little too much. For her, it was an evening of perfect happiness.

At breakfast, she came back to make coffee. She helped Utz with his suitcase to the taxi. Then she climbed upstairs, and listened to the beating of the rain.

The customs men were expecting him at the frontier.

They frisked him, removed the small change from his pockets and, as experts in the art of irritation, appropriated Marta's picnic. Then, finding nothing in his luggage that could be classed as a work of art, they took his copy of 'The Magic Mountain' and a pair of tortoiseshell hairbrushes.

'I suppose,' he muttered as the green caps moved along the corridor, 'they need those for the Museum also.'

After Nuremberg, the rainclouds lifted and the sun came out. He had nothing now to read and so stared from the window at the telegraph wires, the tarred wood gables of the farmhouses, the orchards, the cows in fields of buttercups, and parties of blond-haired children who clung to the barriers of level-crossings and waved their satchels.

The signal-boxes, he noticed, were pitted with bullet-holes. Across the compartment sat a young married couple.

The girl was turning the leaves of an album of

wedding-photos. She was pregnant. She wore a grey smock trimmed with lace. Her bluish legs were unshaven, and her dyed hair dark at the roots.

The boy, Utz was glad to see, was disgusted by her. He looked very ill-at-ease in his American leather flying-jacket, and shuddered whenever she touched him. He was a swarthy, skinny boy with pouting lips and a head of black curls. His nails were stained with nicotine, and he chain-smoked desperately. Was he an Arab, or something? Or a gipsy? Or Italian? Italian, Utz decided, after hearing him speak. She must have had money, and he had been starving. But what a price to pay!

She began to unpack her hamper and Utz began to have second thoughts. He was ravenous. Had he, perhaps, misjudged her? Perhaps she would offer him a share?

He prepared a grateful smile for when the time came. Then, like a dog at the master's table, he watched her swallow a couple of hard-boiled eggs, a schnitzel, a ham sandwich, half a cold chicken and some rounds of garlic sausage. She swilled these down with a bottle of beer, smacked her lips and continued, absent-mindedly, to stuff slices of pumpernickel between them.

The boy hardly touched his food.

Utz could stand the strain no longer. He had come to a decision. He would ask. He would beg. He opened his mouth to say 'Please' – at which the young man tore off a chicken leg and was in the act of handing it across when the girl, shouting 'No! No! No!', slapped him back, and went on peeling an orange.

The smell of orange rind filled the compartment. Ach! What wouldn't he give for an orange! Even a segment of orange! The oranges one got in Prague, scavenged or stolen from one or other of the embassies, were usually shrivelled and tasteless. But this orange dripped its juice over the monster's fingers.

Utz leaned his head against the leathercloth headrest and, closing his eyes, remembered Augustus's aphorism: 'The craving for porcelain is like a craving for oranges.'

The girl called for a napkin, and wiped her fingers. A second orange went the way of the first: then a slice of cheese, a slice of Linzetorte, a Nusstorte, a plum cake. Then she poured herself a coffee from a thermos flask.

She belched. She pestered her husband for a show of affection. He whispered in her ear. Again, Utz summoned an ingratiating smile. But, instead of offering him the last ham sandwich, she fixed him with a glutted stare and, lurching to her feet, chucked it from the window.

Utz watched this little drama draw to its inevitable close and mumbled, in German, loud enough for her to hear:

'It could never have happened in Czechoslovakia.'

At Geneva next morning the man from the bank was waiting on the platform: a rendezvous arranged by the Swiss ambassador in Prague, who, in those days, was 'everyone's friend'.

Utz followed the man's preposterous Tyrolean hat to the lavatory, where he took delivery of a thick manilla envelope containing a wad of Swiss francs, and facsimiles of his share certificates.

He had two hours to kill before the train left for Lyon — and Vichy. He couldn't think of anywhere else to go. He checked his bag at the consigne, and went for breakfast at a café opposite the station. But the coffee was weak, the croissants stale, and the cherry jam tasted of chemical preservative.

He glanced at the other tables. The room was crowded with businessmen on their way to work, burying their faces in the financial columns of the newspapers.

'No,' he told himself. 'I am not enjoying this.'

A t Vichy the hotel had been redecorated, as if to wipe away the stain of having harboured the Laval administration in its rooms. Utz's own room was furnished with reproduction Louis Seize furniture, painted grey. The carpet was blue, and the walls were baby blue with white trim: the décor of the nursery, of the fresh start. On a commode stood a chipped plaster bust of Marie Antoinette, and there were modern engravings: of other bird-brained eighteenth-century ladies.

'No, no,' Utz repeated. 'I am certainly not enjoying this. The French have lost their taste.'

Nor did he enjoy his meetings with Dr Forestier, a man with papery skin and a mouth full of snobbish indiscretions, who had his consulting room in a Gothic house shrouded by paulownias. Nor the immense cream stucco buildings – 'style pâtissier 1900' – stretched out along the Boulevard des États-Unis where the Gestapo had had its headquarters. Nor the mud baths, the frictions, the facials, the pressure-showers. Nor – judging from the drawn, dyspeptic faces of other sufferers – were these celebrated waters in the least beneficial to the health.

He could take no pleasure from the company of the small, aged people – 'ex-colons' whose digestion had been wrecked in Africa or Indo-China – clinging to their raffia-covered 'gobelets de cure' and taking slow, careful steps, out of the rain, under the covered walkway that runs beside the Rue du Parc.

He did not appreciate the gerontophile glint of the masseur – 'a very disturbed young man!' – and hoped that perhaps he was too young. Nor did he care for the ladies of the Grand Établissement Thermal: disciplinarian ladies in white coats and gloves who introduced him to the use of 'les instruments de torture' – remedial machines that Kafka *would* have appreciated – so that he found himself being strapped to a saddle and pummelled, gently but firmly in the intestines, with a pair of leather boxing-gloves.

He winced at the sound of English voices. He averted his eyes from the 'mutilés de guerre': men missing an arm or both legs but playing poker, none the less, on white-painted chairs with perforated seats like cullenders. One evening, after dinner, he had to flee from a lady in tourmaline velvet who spoke, in German, of the Aga Khan.

He became abnormally sensitive to people's stares, especially those of solitary men, who, he imagined, were tailing him.

Who, for example, was that youth in the ill-fitting suit? Hadn't he seen him in Prague? Hanging around the foyer of the Hotel Alkron? No. He had not. The youth was a salesman of sanitary equipment.

Utz pottered round the antique shops and found nothing of interest: a few soapstone Buddhas and dubious Empire clocks. A woman tried to sell him Egyptian amulets, and a pack of tarot cards. At a shop that sold lace, he thought of buying a pinafore to take home to Marta.

'But I won't be going home,' he reflected dismally. 'And anyway they'd steal it at the customs.'

He went to the races, and was bored. He was bored at a concert where they played the 'Suite from Finlandia'. He was desperately bored by the 'Spectacle' at the Grand Théâtre du Casino, which began with 'Les Plus Belles Girls de Paris' – all of them English! – and continued with 'Les Hommes en Crystal' – who were a bunch of fairies smeared with silver paint!

In the interval, he reflected on the absurdity of

his position. Here he was, another middle-aged, Middle European refugee adrift in an unfriendly world! And worse, the most useless of refugees, an aesthete!

After the interval, he had a change of mood.

The curtain rose on Lucienne Boyer, 'La Dame en Bleu': a compact and rounded woman, approaching fifty yet apparently ageless and wearing a dress of dark blue satin, and a blue rose at the apex of her décolleté. She sang number after number at the microphone. Utz's pupils dilated as he gazed, through opera glasses, at her quivering throat. And when she sang 'Parlez-moi d'amour', he got to his feet and shouted 'Bravo! Bravo! Encore!' – and she gave an encore, four of them. And afterwards, after he had watched her leave the theatre with a younger man, he walked home to the Pavillon Sévigné, over cobbled streets slippery with leaves after a hailstorm, his bald head gleaming in the lamplight, swaying slightly and humming the refrain, 'Je vous aime . . . Je vous aime . . . '

Utz had an idea, derived from Russian novels or his parents' love affair at Marienbad, that a spa-town was a place where the unexpected invariably happened.

Two lonely people, brought thither by the accidents of ill-health or unhappiness, would cross paths on their afternoon walk. Their eyes would meet over a bed of municipal marigolds. Drawn by the natural attraction of opposites, they would sit on the same cast-iron seat, and exchange the first stilted sentences. ('Do you come to Vichy often?' 'No. It's my first visit.' 'And mine!') A rapturous evening would end in one or other of their rooms. Either the affair would end in a sad farewell ('No, my dearest, I beg you. Don't come to the station'). Or, when parting seemed inevitable, they would take the drastic decision that would bind them for the rest of their lives.

Utz had come to Vichy with the romantic notion: that, if the decision had to be taken, he would take it.

He hoped . . . he was sure to find among this crowd of solitaries a tender, middle-aged, preferably

73

vulnerable woman who would love him, not for his looks . . . That, alas, was not possible! . . . He had always been ugly, but he did have other qualities.

There had been occasions in the past when a woman had set her sights on him. On each occasion, when intimacy seemed possible, she had uttered the fatal words, 'Oh, you must see his treasures!' – and a cold draught had killed his affection.

No. Anything was better than to be loved for one's things.

But where was she, this elusive female who would fall into his arms? 'Fall' – that was the operative word! Fall, without his having to pursue her. He was tired of pursuing precious objects.

Was she the steel-haired American, widowed or divorced he decided, obviously at Vichy for beauty treatment? Intelligent, of course, but not sympathetic. He mistrusted the acerbic tone with which she ordered her Manhattans from the barman.

Or the soft-voiced creature, Parisian without a doubt, with golden hair and a melting mouth? He saw her first among the morning crowd at the Source des Célestins, moving along the white trellis in a dress of white lace and a hat composed of layers of stiffened chiffon. She had been delicious and would soon be plump. No. Not her. She spent hours in idle chatter in

74

the phone-booth, and came away with a lost look, laughing.

Or the Argentine? 'Grande mangeuse de viande' – or so the waiter said. Utz had stood behind her baccarat table at the Casino, mesmerised by her scarlet talons; by the carefree gestures with which she manoeuvred her chips over the green baize; by the vein in her neck that bulged over her collar of pearls. Not her either! She was joined by her husband.

And then he saw her, one afternoon, in the lobby: a tall, white-limbed woman in tennis whites, her dark hair plaited in a coif, slipping a cover over her racquet and thanking, in a tone of firm finality, the over-eager pro for his lesson.

Utz heard her conversing in French, although he thought – or was he imagining this? – that he detected a Slavic resonance in her accent. She was not the athletic type: there was an oriental torpor in her movements. She might have been Turkish, this 'femme en forme de violon' with her apple-blossom cheeks, her dimples, her quivering forelip and slanting green eyes. She wasn't beautiful by modern standards: the kind of woman they once bred for the seraglio.

'But she has to be Russian,' he reflected. 'Russian, certainly. With a touch of Tartar?'

She was no longer young, and she seemed very sad.

He spent the rest of the afternoon in a state of feverish excitement, waiting for her to re-emerge from the lift, and attempting to compose a history for her. He imagined the downward spiral of émigré life: the rented apartment in Monaco; later, when the jewels ran out, the lodgings in Paris where her father drove a taxi and played chess after hours. To pay for his medical bills, she had sacrificed herself to the businessman who kept her in a certain style, but also kept a younger mistress. He had taken the mistress to the Riviera and sent his wife, who was childless, to Vichy.

She came downstairs before dinner, still alone, wearing a spotted grey dress and white open-toed shoes. And when Utz saw her little dog, a Sealyham, trailing at her heels, he called to mind the lady in the Chekhov tale and felt for certain the meeting must happen.

He followed her at a distance into the park beside the Allier, stationing himself on a bench which she was almost sure to pass, inhaling the odour of lilac and philadelphus.

'Viens, Maxi! Viens! Viens!' – he heard her calling the dog; and when she came to a choice of forking paths, she chose the path that led towards him.

'Bonsoir, Madame!' Utz smiled, and was about to call 'Maxi!' to the dog. The woman gave a start, and quickened her pace.

He continued to sit, miserably listening to the crunch of her footfalls on the gravel. At dinner, she passed his table and looked the other way.

He saw her again in the morning, in the passenger seat of a silver sports car, her arms around the neck of the man at the wheel.

He asked the concierge who she was and was told she was Belgian.

He turned his attention to food.

On his first day at Vichy he had bought, from a bookshop in the Rue Clemenceau, a 'gastronomic guide' to the region. He had always cared for his stomach, always befriended chefs.

How often, in the war years, especially in moments of terror, did he recollect the pleasures of the table! The day the Gestapo took him for questioning, he had been unable to focus on the abstractions of death or deportation: only on the memory of a particular plate of haricots verts, at a restaurant by a white road in Provence.

Later, during the worst of the winter shortages, the months of cabbage, cabbage, cabbage and potatoes, he comforted himself with the thought that, when sanity returned and the frontiers were open, he would eat once again in France.

He studied the guide with the fastidious dedication he usually reserved for porcelain-hunting: where to find the best 'quenelles aux écrevisses', the best 'cervelas truffé' or a 'poulet à la vessie'. Or the desserts — the 'bourriouls', 'bougnettes', 'flaugnardes', 'fouasses'. (One could hear the gas in those names!) Or the rare white wine of Château Grillet, which was said to taste of vine flowers and almonds — and behave like a capricious young woman.

Putting his new-found knowledge to the test, he reserved a table at a restaurant beside the Allier.

The day was warm and sunny: sufficiently warm to eat outside on the terrace, under an awning of green-and-white striped canvas that flapped lazily in the breeze. There were three wine glasses set at each place. He watched the reflections of the poplars z-bending across the river, and the sand-martins skimming over its surface. On the far bank, fishermen and their families had spread their picnics on the grass.

The waiters were fussing over a 'prince of gastronomes' who was paying his annual visit. He had come in after Utz, flushed crimson in the face and perambulating his stomach before him. He tucked his napkin inside his collar, and prepared to plough through an eight-course luncheon.

At last, when the menu came, Utz gave a grateful smile to the maître d'hôtel.

He ran his eye over the list of specialities. He chose. He changed his mind. He chose again: an artichoke soup, trout 'Mont Doré' and sucking-pig 'à la lyonnaise'.

'Et comme vin, monsieur?'

'What would you suggest?'

The wine-waiter, taking Utz for an ignoramus, pointed to two of the more expensive bottles on the list: a Montrachet and a Clos Margeot.

'No Château Grillet?'

'Non, monsieur.'

'Very well,' Utz acquiesced obediently. 'Whatever you recommend.'

The meal failed to match his expectations. Not that he could fault its quality or presentation: but the soup, although exquisite, seemed savourless; the trout was smothered in a sauce of Gruyère cheese, and the sucking-pig was stuffed with something else.

He looked again, enviously, at the picnickers on the opposite shore. A young mother rushed to save her child, who had crawled to the water's edge. He would like to be with them: to share their coarse, home-made pies that surely tasted of something! Or had he lost his own sense of taste?

The bill was larger than he expected. He left in a bad mood. He felt bloated, and a little dizzy.

He had also come to a depressing conclusion: that luxury is only luxurious under adverse conditions.

In the afternoon the clouds came up and it began to rain. He lay down in his room and read some pages of a novel by Gide. His French was inadequate: he lost the thread of the narrative.

He put the book aside, and stared vacantly at the chandelier.

Why, he asked himself, when he had steeled himself to the horrors of war and revolution, should the free world present so frightening an abyss? Why, each time he sank onto the mattress, did he have the sensation of falling, like the elevator, through the floors of the hotel? In Prague he slept soundly. Why did sleep elude him here?

He would lie awake and fret over his finances. In Czechoslovakia he had no finances to speak of: or none that he could lay his hands on. Now, at two and three in the morning, he would spread his share-certificates over the bedspread and tot up the figures of his portfolio, searching for a flaw, a mistake; trying to explain why, in a rising stock-market, his fortune in Switzerland had shrunk. Why, with enormous sums invested, were the sums on paper so small? Someone, somewhere was cheating him. Taking advantage while his back was turned! But who? And how?

From the same bookshop he had bought a pocket atlas of the world; and, leafing through its pages, he tried to imagine the country he would like to live in. Or rather, the country that would make him least unhappy.

Switzerland? Italy? France? Three possibilities. None of them inviting. Germany? Never. The break had been final. England? Not after the Dresden raid. The United States? Impossible. The noise would depress him dreadfully. Prague, after all, was a city where you heard the snowflakes falling. Australia? He had never been attracted by the colonies. Argentina? He was too old to tango.

The more he considered the alternatives, the clearer the solution seemed to him. Not that he would be happy in Czechoslovakia. He would be harassed, menaced, insulted. He would have to grovel. He would have to agree with every word they said. He would mouth their meaningless, ungrammatical formulae. He would learn to 'live within the lie'.

But Prague was a city that suited his melancholic temperament. A state of tranquil melancholy was all one could aspire to these days! And for the first time, grudgingly, he felt he could admire his Czech compatriots: not for their decision to vote in a Marxist government . . . Any fool knew by now that Marxism was a winded philosophy! He admired the abstemiousness of their choice.

He continued to stare at the idiotic chandelier, turning over in his mind the most troublesome question of all.

He was desperately homesick, yet hadn't given a thought for the porcelains. He could only think of Marta, alone, in the apartment.

He felt remorse for having left her: the poor darling who adored him; who would lay down her life for him; her passionate heart that beat for him, and him only, concealed under a mask of reserve, of duty and obedience.

He had thought of taking her to the West. But she spoke no language other than Czech, and a few words of German. No. She'd be . . . he groped for the appropriate cliché . . . she'd be a fish out of water.

He remembered the times when, breathless from climbing the stairs, the snowflakes twinkling on her fox fur hat, she would return from a successful deal on the black market. Her capacity for bargaining was prodigious, even with a single dollar bill.

She would stand for hours in a food queue: nothing mattered if the object of her quest would bring him pleasure.

Some days, she filled her shopping-bag with muddy potatoes. No one knew better that the type of policeman who would pry among her purchases was the type to mind muddying his hands. And afterwards, when she had dumped the potatoes in the sink, she would pull from the bottom of the bag a pheasant or a hare that someone had brought in from the country.

Her contacts with the countryside functioned like the bush-telegraph.

'Where did you get those eggs?' he'd ask, as she rushed a golden soufflé to the table.

'A woman brought them,' she would answer vaguely.

She understood, by instinct, why he insisted on the details: the sauce in a sauceboat; the starching of shirt-cuffs; the Sèvres coffee cups on Sunday – for a coffee composed of roasted barley and chicory! – the minor acts of style to demonstrate that he had not given in.

He recognised her attentions as the tokens of her love. He could not bring himself to thank her: nor would she have wanted this.

Their happiest time together was the mushroom season, towards the end of August, after the first late summer cloudbursts. They would catch the early morning train to Tábor; the bus to Céske Krížove;

and from there, taking care to avoid the big house, take their picnic into the woods.

Mushrooms, he said, were the only reason for revisiting the scenes of his childhood.

He and Marta were like children at play, oblivious of caste or class, as they called to one another through the pine trunks: 'Look what I've found . . . ! Look what I've found . . . !' – a russet-cowled boletus, an edible agaric, or a cluster of chanterelles pushing their orange caps above a carpet of moss.

No one but they and a few woodcutters knew the clearing where, as master of the estate, he had sawn himself a rustic table and seat: from the timbers of a beech tree that had been split by lightning.

They would spread their finds on the table, gills uppermost, discarding those which were spongy or grub-ridden, cleaning off the larger lumps of earth yet leaving the odd pine-needle or a scrap of fern frond.

'Don't clean them too much,' she would scold him. 'A bit of dirt makes them taste much better.'

Then she fried them in butter over a spirit stove, and stirred in a dollop of cream.

One day, on their way back to Prague, they stopped in the town square at Tábor where local mushroom fanciers had set up stalls, under awnings of sackcloth to prevent the sun from shrivelling their treasures.

A hubbub of cheerful voices greeted him. A peasant woman, a white headscarf wrapped low over her weather-beaten face, stood up and cried, 'Look! It's the master come back!' He watched his old doctor, a mushroom fanatic, bartering furiously with a professional mycologist from the university over some very rare specimen. And there was Marianna Palach! – the laundrywoman, wizened to a husk now, who none the less went mushrooming, and had set up shop.

Everyone in the market was laughing, haggling, giving, taking, proving beyond all doubt, whatever the zealots had to say, that the business of trade was one of life's most natural and enjoyable pleasures, no more to be abolished than the act of falling in love . . .

'What am I doing here?' Utz roused himself from his daydream.

He looked at his wristwatch. He was late for dinner. He knotted his tie in front of the bathroom mirror. He trimmed his moustache. (I still cannot be certain if I'm imagining a moustache.) He examined his stubborn little mouth, and said, 'No!'

He was not going to join the flow of exiles. He would not sit complaining in rented rooms. He knew that anti-Communist rhetoric was as deadly as its Communist counterpart. He would not give up his country. Not for them!

He would go back. But he knew that, once he got back, the porcelains would re-exert the power of snobbery. The ladies of the Dresden court would turn their vitreous smiles on Marta, dismissing her to the kitchenette — where she would sit, patiently, in her shabby maid's uniform and black stockings with holes at the knee.

He went down to dinner in the restaurant. At a table nearby, a pair of married couples were engaged in a merciless argument over the merits or otherwise of an 'Alaska', an 'Île flottante' or an 'Omelette norvégienne'. The women had rasping voices. The men were fat and wore rings.

Their menu seemed to consist entirely of desserts: a Mont Blanc, profiterolles, a fruit salad, a tarte Tatin, a raspberry ice with chantilly, a chocolate cake with more chantilly . . .

'This is disgusting,' Utz muttered. 'No. It is impossible I should stay here.'

He rose from the table and told the receptionist he would be leaving on the morning train.

It depressed him, on crossing the Czech frontier, to see the lines of barbed wire and sentry-boxes. But he noted, with a certain relief, that there were no more advertising billboards.

Utz was one of those rare individuals who, throughout the Cold War, persisted in the illusion that the Iron Curtain was essentially flimsy. Because of his investments in the West — and powers of persuasion that mystified both himself and the bureaucrats of Prague — he succeeded in keeping a foot in both camps.

Year after year, he made the ritual pilgrimage to Vichy. By the end of April, his resentment against the regime rose to boiling-point: for its incompetence, nothing more — he considered it common to complain of collectivisation. By April, too, he felt acute claustrophobia, from having spent the winter months in close proximity to the adoring Marta: to say nothing of the boredom, verging on fury, that came from living those months with lifeless porcelain.

Before leaving, he would make a resolution never, ever to return — while at the same time making arrangements for his return – and would set off for Switzerland in the best of spirits.

The journey was always the same: to Geneva, for meetings with his bankers and an antiquaire: on to Vichy, and to Vichy only, to taste the waters, to breathe the fresh air of freedom that rapidly went stale, and order more expensive meals which would disgust him.

He would then bolt for home like a man pursued by demons.

One year, he went to Paris for the week-end: but that completely upset his equilibrium.

These arrangements suited no one except himself. For Marta, his absence was a time of torment, almost of mourning. For the officials who issued his exit visa – men who seriously believed that so incurable a decadent belonged in Vichy, America or some such corrupted place, and who prided themselves on their leniency in letting him go – his return was the act of a madman.

It was equally puzzling to a succession of consuls in the French and Swiss embassies. Accustomed, as they were, to think of Czechoslovakia as a country from which people of Utz's standing fled, in an east-westerly direction, the idea that any normal person might prefer home to exile seemed excessively perverse: an act of ingratitude. Or was there some sinister motive? Was M. Utz a spy?

No. He was not a spy. As he explained to me in the course of our afternoon stroll, Czechoslovakia was a pleasant place to live, providing one had the possibility of leaving. At the same time he admitted, with a self-deprecating smile, that his severe case of Porzellankrankheit prevented him from leaving for good. The collection held him prisoner.

'And, of course, it has ruined my life!'

In an unguarded moment he also confessed to a secret cache of Meissen, stored in a numbered safe deposit, in the Union de Banques Suisses in Geneva.

Whenever his share prices rose above a certain level, he siphoned off a sum of money to pay for yet another object: the calculation being that if, over the years, the cache in Geneva approached the quality, not necessarily the quantity, of the collection in Prague, he might once again be tempted to emigrate.

One year – I believe it was 1963 – the New York dealer, Dr Marius Frankfurter, made a special trip to

Vichy to offer Utz a piece of porcelain that was quite outside his usual range: a model known as 'The Spaghetti Eater', made not at Meissen, but at the CapodiMonte factory in Naples.

In the same baby blue bedroom, Dr Frankfurter unwrapped the object from its multiple layers of tissue-paper and set it on the commode, with the reverence of a priest exhibiting the Host. Utz could hardly help comparing its pearly glaze with the warted epidermis of the dealer. But that was life! The ugliest men loved the most beautiful things.

'So?' said Dr Frankfurter.

'So,' Utz pursed his lips.

The object was adorable. He was not going to say so.

A figure of Pulchinella – the 'Charlie Chaplin' of the Italian Comedy – sat lounging in a kind of invalid chair, wearing a collarette of green lace over a loose linen shirt, and a conical white hat like that of a dancing dervish. At his side, a Neapolitan lad, in a scarlet cap and purple breeches, was feeding him from a chamber pot.

Utz was particularly taken with the coils of spaghetti, poised either to plunge into Pulchinella's mouth – or into one of his cavernous nostrils.

But the price! Even Dr Frankfurter seemed in awe

of the price, and could only bring himself to mention it in a whisper.

'Well,' said Utz, after recovering from the initial shock. 'I've never bought a piece of Italian porcelain in my life. How would I know it was genuine?'

'Tschenuin?' Dr Frankfurter spluttered.

Of course it was genuine! And Utz, of course, knew it was genuine. He was simply playing for time.

But the Doctor was aggrieved. He threatened to re-wrap the piece in its tissue: only to relent and reel off a tremendous pedigree of the noble Italian families to whom it had belonged — names that meant no more to Utz than a list of railway stations from Ventimiglia to Bari — until, in a crescendo of name-dropping, he arrived at Queen Maria Amalia herself.

'Oh?' said Utz. 'It belonged to her, did it?'

For he knew — and Dr Frankfurter knew he knew — that, before becoming Queen of Naples, this plain and pox-pitted woman had been a Princess of Saxony, and was the granddaughter of Augustus the Strong.

It was she who, in 1739, had founded the Naples factory, hardly a stone's throw from the Palace, as a project to divert her Germanic energies into something useful.

Utz made his mind up. 'The Spaghetti Eater' would

have to be bought: if only to rescue it from Dr Frankfurter's sweaty hands. But he would not give in without a fight!

The Doctor — Doctor in what was a mystery — took the line that he was offering the object as a mark of special friendship. He showed Utz a book in which it was illustrated; a chemical analysis of the paste, and a bill from an auction sale in 1949.

'And the price is a "prix d'ami",' he said, not once but repeatedly. He could sell it in America ten times over. For twice the amount!

'Why don't you?' Utz called his bluff.

His tactic was to pooh-pooh the productions of the Naples factory. The object, he insisted, was not really in his line — although he would like it in the collection 'for the purpose of comparative study'.

The day was overcast and drizzly. He looked from the window at the trees of the Parc de l'Allier. He had counted on being able to knock a third off the price. Dr Frankfurter was obstinate as a mule.

Five times, the dealer stalked off down the corridor with the box under his arm. Five times Utz called him back. Once, they got as far as the lobby, where the other guests were astonished to see two middle-aged gentlemen jabbering in German at the tops of their voices.

Eventually, they struck a deal: out of sheer exhaustion!

There followed a hasty packing of suitcases and a train journey to Geneva — where Utz had promised to withdraw the sum in cash. Neither spoke. Dr Frankfurter was congealed with anxiety that Utz might wriggle out of the bargain. Utz was sunk in gloom that he hadn't gone on bargaining further.

They shook hands, frostily, on the steps of the Union de Banques Suisses.

'So, till next year!' said Dr Frankfurter.

'Till next year!' Utz nodded, and turned his back on the taxi.

He returned to the bank, to examine his purchase alone.

He entered the familiar underground corridor where the lines of stainless-steel deposit boxes seemed to stretch away, like railway lines, to vanishing point. Who knew what treasures they contained? Enough to fill a museum, he chuckled. With a lot of expensive junk!

At intervals along the corridor there were tables, lit with anglepoise lamps, where customers could gloat over their possessions. A woman in a red wig sat fingering an emerald bracelet. Beyond her, a Lebanese dealer in antiquities was protesting the authenticity of a corroded bronze animal. His client, an excitable young man in spectacles, denounced it as a fake.

Utz heard the young man say 'Archifaux!' – and trembled.

Perhaps Dr Frankfurter had also sold him a fake? His fingers tore at the tissue-paper. He scrutinised the object with a pocket-magnifying glass – and breathed again.

'Out of the question! It has to be genuine!'

The spaghetti was a marvel. Pulchinella's nose was a marvel. The enamels surpassed in subtlety the colours of Meissen. He had done the right thing. It was cheap. Cheap, when one thought of it. Besides, he adored it! And when the time came to return it to its stainless-steel coffin, he hesitated.

'No,' he told himself. 'I cannot leave it here.'

Thus, when others were bent on smuggling out of Czechoslovakia, in diplomatic bags or a foreign friend's suitcase, any article of value they could lay their hands on – a snuff-box, an ancestral decoration, or a vermeil dessert service, fork by fork – Utz embarked on the opposite course.

'I smuggled it *in*,' he whispered.

He was standing in the middle of the room, roughly equidistant from the lynx and the turkey-cock. I rose to join him, almost barking my shin on the corner of the Mies van der Rohe table. 'The Spaghetti Eater' stood on the central shelf, to the right of Madame de Pompadour.

'Marta,' Utz called.

The maid came in with a fresh plate of canapés: but the moment she took stock of our position, she withdrew to the kitchenette and, reaching for a couple of aluminium saucepans, began to bang them together like cymbals.

'They cannot hear us now,' he said, standing on tiptoe. He had put his mouth to my ear.

'Are they listening?'

'All the time!' he sniggered. 'There is a microphone in this wall. One in that wall. Another in the ceiling, and I know not where else. They listen, listen, listen to everything. But this everything is too much for them. So they *hear* nothing!'

The saucepans clattered like the noise of a pneumatic drill. From under our feet there was another noise, of a stick or broom-handle being thumped against the ceiling of the apartment below, presumably by the furious soprano.

'Some days,' he continued, 'they call me and say "Utz, what are you doing over there? Breaking porcelains?" "No," I say. "That is Marta cooking supper." One of them, I have to say it, is a very humorous person. We are friends.'

'Friends?'

'Telephone friends. Wc now learn to like each other. That is correct, no?'

'If you say so.'

'So I say it.'

'Good.'

'Good,' he repeated. 'Now I will ask you questions.'

Bang! . . .   Bang! . . .   Bang! . . .   Bang! . . .
Bang! . . .   Bang! . . .

'How much would cost today a Kaendler harlequin in auction sale in London?'

'I've no idea,' I said.

'Really?' he frowned. 'You know porcelains so nicely and you don't know prices.'

'I'd be guessing.'

'Go on,' he giggled. 'Guess it.'

'Ten thousand pounds.'

'Ten thousand? How much that in dollars?'

'Not quite thirty thousand.'

'You are right, sir!' Utz closed his eyes. 'Last one sold twenty-seven thousand dollars. That was in America. Parke-Bernet Galleries. But it was broken as to the hand.'

Bang! . . . Bang! . . . Bang! . . . Bang! . . . Bang! . . .

'So how much the Augustus Rex vases?'

I cannot recall the size of the figure I mentioned. Certainly, I thought it high enough to give him pleasure. But he looked dismayed, bit his lip, and said, 'More! More!'

A single vase had fetched more in Paris, at the Hôtel Drouot. This was a complete garniture, without a crack or blemish anywhere.

Little by little, I was drawn into the spirit of the guessing game. I learned, with practice, to come up with the figures he wanted to hear and, in this way, I valued the bittern, the rhino, the Brühl tureen, Fröhlich and Schmeidl, the Pompadour and even 'The Spaghetti Eater'.

We stood for almost an hour. Utz would point to an object on the shelves. Marta would bang her saucepans. I would cup both hands around his ear, stickying my fingers on his brilliantine, and whispering higher and higher prices.

From time to time, he let out a squeal of joy. Finally, he said, 'So how much the whole collection?'

'Millions.'

'Ha! You are right,' said Utz. 'I am a porcelain millionaire.'

The clatter of saucepans died away: to be followed, a few minutes later, by the sound of sizzling fat.

'You will eat with me?' he said.

'I will,' I said. 'Thank you. Do you mind if I use your bathroom?'

Utz pretended not to hear.

'Do you mind if I use your bathroom?'

He flinched. His face became contorted with a nervous tic. He fumbled with a cufflink, shot an agonised glance in the direction of the kitchenette – and pulled himself together.

'Ja! Ja! You may do that!' he stuttered, and ushered me, past a double bed, into an immaculate bathroom with a frieze of green-and-lilac jugendstil tiles and a bathtub on which the enamel had worn thin.

I closed the door behind me – and saw an astonishing garment.

Suspended from a hook there was a dressing-gown: but instead of a plaid or a camel-hair dressing-gown, this was a robe of quilted, peach-coloured art silk, with appliqué roses on the shoulders and a collar of matching pink ostrich plumes.

The scenario suggested by this unexpected costume set my imagination into turmoil.

I pulled the lavatory chain. Outside, above the rush and gurgle of the water, I heard Utz and Marta remonstrating, in Czech.

He was waiting to hustle me out of the bedroom. I was not to be hustled.

I paused to admire an eighteenth-century engraving, of a fireworks display at the Zwinger. I saw a photograph of Utz's father. I saw his illustrious decoration on its mount of black velvet. I saw a 'Venetian' blackamoor bed-table and, on it, a book by Schnitzler, and one by Stefan Zweig. I saw a large container of talcum-powder – or was it face-powder? – in front of the dressing-mirror. I saw three other unexpected items: a rosary, a crucifix and a scapular of the Infant of Prague.

The frilly lace lampshade had been singed by its electric light bulb. The flounced pink curtains and pink satin eiderdown – both of which had seen better days – gave the room an atmosphere of musty, rather coarse femininity.

I looked at Utz afresh in the light of this discovery. I looked at his shiny scalp. Was there perhaps, hidden under the skirts of the dressing-table, a wig?

He was unable to look me in the eye. Instead, he tinkered with the gramophone and put on a record: a keyboard sonata by the Saxon court composer, Jan Dismas Zelenka.

The maid reappeared and laid two places on the glass-topped table, banging down the knives and forks with a show of bad temper. She turned her back, and returned with a larger Meissen dish on which were arranged some pork chops, sauerkraut and dumplings in gravy.

Utz ate with dulled concentration, pausing now and then to mouth a little bread, sip a little wine, but scarcely saying a word. He blinked at me: apparently furious with himself for having invited this inquisitive foreigner who had disturbed his peace of mind and might, in the long run, cause trouble.

He cringed whenever the maid showed her face. After helping himself to seconds, he began to relax.

He cut a cube of meat, impaled it, held it in the air, and addressed me, pedantically:

'Each time I see a piece of pork on my fork, I must remind myself that "pork" and "porcelain" are the same word.'

'Really?' I said. 'How's that?'

'Really, you don't know it?'

'Really not.'

'So I will explain.'

He reached for one of the shelves and handed me a small white cowrie shell, an ordinary specimen of 'Cypraea moneta'. Did its shape, by any chance, remind me of a pig?

'Why not?'

'Good,' he said. 'We agree on that one also.'

Cowries, he went on, were used as currency in Africa and Asia where they were traded for ivory, gold, slaves or other marketable commodities. Marco Polo called them 'porcelain shells': 'porcella' in Italian was the word for 'little sow'.

He let out a perfect hiccough, probably caused by the sauerkraut.

'I apologise,' he said.

'Don't mention it.'

He then produced, as if from nowhere, a bottle of translucent white porcelain which dated from the epoch of Kublai Khan. He had bought it in Paris before the War. Wouldn't I agree that its glaze resembled that of a cowrie?

'I would.'

'Thank you.'

His next exhibit was the photo of an almost identical bottle in the Treasury of St Mark's: an object which was said to have arrived in Venice in the bags of Marco Polo himself.

'So now you understand about "pork" and "porcelain"?'

'I think so,' I said.

Chinese porcelain, he continued, was one of those legendary substances, like unicorn horn or alchemical gold, from which men hoped to drink the Fountain of Youth. A porcelain cup was said to crack or discolour if poison were poured into it.

Marta cleared the table, served coffee, and opened a box of Carlsbad plums. Utz hiccoughed again and bombarded me with a flood of questions.

Had I been to China? Had I read the letters of Father Matteo Ricci? Or Father d'Entrecolles' description of porcelain manufacture? How serious, really, was my understanding of Chinese porcelain? Under the Sung? The Ming? The Ch'ing?

From the seventeenth century, he said, the Emperors of China had made a colossal impact on the European imagination. They were thought to be very wise and to live to a very great age, dispensing arbitrary, impartial justice according to laws derived from Earth and Heaven. They drank from porcelain. They built pagodas of porcelain. The smooth and lustrous surface of porcelain corresponded to the smooth, unwrinkled surface of themselves. Porcelain was *their* material – as gold was the material of the Roi Soleil.

'And even today,' Utz added flippantly, 'our Soviet friends are never too poor to pay for gilding.'

'Then would you say', I interrupted, 'that your Augustus's porcelain-mania was conditioned by legends of the Yellow Emperor?'

'Say it? Of course, I would say it! And not only kings loved porcelain. Philosophers also! Leibniz was crazy for porcelain!'

Leibniz – who had believed this world was the best of all possible worlds – believed that porcelain was its best material.

The maid stood motionless in the hallway, fixing her employer with a hostile stare, as if requiring him to end the interview. He took no notice:

'Now will you look please at these two little persons?'

'These' were a pair of identical statuettes of Augustus the Strong, wreathed as a Roman Emperor and standing like Tweedledum and Tweedledee amid the Dresden ladies. They were not modelled with much sophistication – yet had the concentrated energy of an African fetish.

One was made of red Böttger ware, the so-called 'jasper-porcelain'. The other was white.

'Tell me,' said Utz, 'what you know about Böttger.'

'Not much,' I replied. 'He began as an alchemist, and then he invented porcelain.'

'He *may* have invented porcelain. But even that is not so sure.'

I reached for my notebook. He reeled off a synopsis of Böttger's career.

Johannes Böttger is born in 1682, in Schleiz in Thuringia, the son of an official of the Mint. After a childhood in the workshop of his grandfather, a goldsmith, he is apprenticed to a Berlin apothecary by the name of Zorn.

He studies books on alchemy: the Blessed Raymond Lúll, Basilius Valentinus, Paracelsus and Van Helmont's 'Aphorismi Chemici' in which alchemical substances are listed as the Ruby Lion, Black Raven, Green Dragon, and White Lily.

He convinces himself that gold and silver are matured in the bowels of the earth, out of red and white arsenic. One night, his fellow apprentices find him in Zorn's laboratory half-asphyxiated by arsenic fumes.

Among the customers of the pharmacy is a Greek mendicant monk, Lascaris, who is reputed to possess the Red Tincture, or 'Ruby Lion', a grain of which will transmute lead into gold.

The monk falls for the boy.

Böttger obtains a phial of the tincture and performs his first 'successful' transmutation, in the lodgings of a student friend. The second 'successful' experiment takes place in front of Zorn and other sceptical witnesses.

The ladies of Berlin find the young alchemist irresistible. His reputation spreads: to King Frederick William, the 'Giant Lover', who obtains a specimen of the gold from Frau Zorn – and issues a warrant for Böttger's arrest.

Böttger escapes to Wittenberg: a dependency of Augustus the Strong.

In November 1701 the Kings of Prussia and Saxony

hold military manoeuvres along their borders. Which of these indigent sovereigns shall possess the gold-maker? Böttger – like a fugitive nuclear physicist – is escorted to Dresden under armed guard.

In the Jungfernbastei, one of several prisons he will occupy over the next thirteen years, he dines off silver plate, keeps a pet monkey and, in a secret laboratory, sets to work on the 'arcanum universale' or Philosopher's Stone.

By 1706 the Saxon Treasury is exhausted: from the cost of the Swedish War and the King's compulsive purchases of Chinese porcelain. Augustus, infuriated by Böttger's failure, threatens to remove him to another laboratory: the torture chamber.

Böttger meets Ehrenfried Walther, Graf von Tschirnhaus. This outstanding chemist, the friend of Leibniz, is on the way to discovering the secret of 'true' porcelain, but cannot devise a kiln sufficiently hot to fuse the glaze and the body. He recognises Böttger's talents, and asks for his co-operation. The alchemist, to save his skin, agrees.

Over the door of this workshop Böttger hangs a notice:

God, Our Creator
Has turned a Goldmaker into a Potter.

In 1708 he delivers to Augustus the first specimens of red porcelain and, in the following year, the white.

In 1710 the Royal Saxon Porcelain Manufactory is founded at Meissen and begins work on a commercial scale. 'Arcanum' – a word usually employed by alchemists – is the official term for the chemical composition of the paste. The formula is declared a State secret. Almost at once, the secret is betrayed by Böttger's assistant – and sold to Vienna.

In 1719 Böttger dies, of drink, depression, delusion and chemical poisoning.

During the German inflation of 1923 the Dresden banks issue emergency money, in red and white 'Böttger' porcelain.

U tz had some specimens of this 'funny money' to show me. He dropped them, like chocolates, into the palm of my hand.

'Very interesting,' I said.

'But now I tell you something more interesting.'

Most porcelain experts, he continued, interpreted Böttger's discovery as the utilitarian by-product of alchemy – like Paracelsus's mercurial cure for syphilis.

He did not agree. He felt it was foolish to attribute to former ages the materialist concerns of this one. Alchemy, except among its more banal practitioners, was never a technique for multiplying wealth ad infinitum. It was a mystical exercise. The search for gold and the search for porcelain had been facets of an identical quest: to find the substance of immortality.

As for himself, he had taken up alchemical studies on the advice of Zikmund Kraus: both as a field for his polymathic impulses, and as a means of elevating his 'porcelain mania' onto a metaphysical plane: so that if the Communists took the collection, he would none the less continue to possess it.

Utz had read his Jung, his Goethe, Michael Maier, the ramblings of Dr Dee and Pernéty's 'Dictionnaire Mytho-Hermétique'. He knew all there was to be known about the 'mother of alchemy', Mary the Jewess, a third-century chemist who is said to have invented the retort.

Chinese alchemists, he went on, used to teach that gold was the 'body of the gods'. Christians, with their insistence on simplification, equated it with the Body of Christ: the perfect, untarnishable substance, an elixir which could snatch one from the Jaws of Death. But was this gold gold as we knew it? Or an 'aurum potabile', to be drunk?

Jewels and metals, he said, were thought to mature in the womb of the earth. As a pallid foetus matured into a creature of flesh and blood, so crystals reddened into rubies, silver into gold. An alchemist believed he could speed up the process with the help of the two 'tinctures': the White Stone, with which base metals were converted into silver; the Red Stone which was 'the last work of alchemy' – gold itself! Did I understand that?

'I hope so,' I said weakly.

He shifted to a different tack.

What did I know of the homunculus of Paracelsus? Nothing? Well, Paracelsus had claimed to create a homunculus from a fermentation of blood, sperm and urine.

'A kind of test-tube baby?'

'More probably a kind of golem.'

'I knew we'd get back to golems,' I said.

'We have,' he agreed.

Would I now please reflect on the fact that Nebuchadnezzar had the burning fiery furnace heated to seven times its normal temperature when he put in Shadrach, Meshach and Abednego?

'Seven times, I ask you!' Utz waved his hands in the air.

'Are you trying to tell me that Shadrach, Meshach and Abednego were ceramic figures?'

'They could have been,' he answered. 'They certainly survived the fire.'

'I see,' I said. 'So you *do* think the porcelains are alive?'

'I do and I do not,' he sniggered. 'Porcelains die in the fire, and then they come alive again. The kiln, you must understand, is Hell. The temperature for firing porcelain is 1,450 degrees centigrade.'

'Yes,' I said.

Utz's flights of fancy made me feel quite dizzy. He appeared to be saying that the earliest European porcelain – Böttger's red ware and white ware – corresponded to the red and white tinctures of the alchemists. To a superstitious old roué like Augustus, the manufacture of porcelain was an approach to the Philosopher's Stone.

If this were so: if, to the eighteenth-century imagination, porcelain was not just another exotic, but a magical and talismanic substance – the substance of longevity, of potency, of invulnerability – then it was easier to understand why the King would stuff a palace with forty thousand pieces. Or guard the 'arcanum' like a secret weapon. Or swap the six hundred giants.

Porcelain, Utz concluded, was the antidote to decay.

The illusion was, of course, shattered by Frederick the Great who simply loaded the contents of the Meissen factory onto ox-carts and sent it, as booty, to Berlin.

'But Frederick,' Utz fluttered his eyelids, ' . . . and with all that musical talent! . . . was really an absolute philistine!'

The room was almost in darkness. It was a warm night, and a soft breeze ruffled the net curtains. On the carpet, the animals from the Japanese Palace shimmered like lumps of phosphorescence.

'Marta!' he called. 'A light please!'

The maid came in with a Meissen candlestick, and set it carefully in the centre of the table. She put a match to the candle. Innumerable points of flame were reflected in the walls.

Utz changed the record on the gramophone: to the recitative of Zerbinetta and Harlequin from

Strauss's 'Ariadne auf Naxos'.

I have said that Utz's face was 'waxy in texture', but now in the candlelight its texture seemed like melted wax. I looked at the ageless complexion of the Dresden ladies. Things, I reflected, are tougher than people. Things are the changeless mirror in which we watch ourselves disintegrate. Nothing is more age-ing than a collection of works of art.

One by one, he lifted the characters of the Commedia from the shelves, and placed them in the pool of light where they appeared to skate over the glass of the table, pivoting on their bases of gilded foam, as if they would forever go on laughing, whirling, improvising.

Scaramouche would strum on his guitar.

Brighella would liberate people's purses.

The Captain would swagger childishly like all army officers.

The Doctor would kill his patient in order to rid him of his disease.

The coils of spaghetti would be eternally poised above Pulchinella's nostrils.

Pantaloon would gloat over his money-bags.

The Innamorata, like all transvestites everywhere, would be mobbed on his way to the theatre.

Columbine would be endlessly in love with Harlequin – 'absolutely mad to trust him'.

And Harlequin . . . *The* Harlequin . . . the arch-improviser, the zany, trickster, master of the volte-face . . . would forever strut in his variegated plumage, grin through his orange mask, tiptoe into bedrooms, sell nappies for the children of the Grand Eunuch, dance in the teeth of catastrophe . . . Mr Chameleon himself!

And I realised, as Utz pivoted the figure in the candlelight, that I had misjudged him; that he, too, was dancing; that, for him, this world of little figures was the real world. And that, compared to them, the Gestapo, the Secret Police and other hooligans were creatures of tinsel. And the events of this sombre century – the bombardments, blitzkriegs, putsches, purges – were, so far as he was concerned, so many 'noises off'.

'And now,' he said, 'we shall go. We shall go for a walk.'

O n my way out, I thanked Marta for cooking supper. A wan smile passed across her face. Without getting off her stool, she inclined her torso stiffly from the waist.

It was a very warm and sultry night, and moths were whirling round the street lamps. In Old Town Square, crowds of young people had congregated at the foot of the Jan Hus Memorial. They seemed fresh and full of vigour: the boys in white open-necked shirts; the girls in old-fashioned cotton dresses.

The stars came out behind the spires of the Týn Church and, to peals of organ music, more people began to file through the arcades of the Divinity School, on their way from Mass. 'Prague Spring' was almost a year away: yet I remember an atmosphere of optimism. I remember being taken aback when Utz turned on me, and bared his teeth.

'I hate this city,' he said.

'Hate it? How can you hate it? You said it was a beautiful city.'

'I hate it. I hate it.'

'Things will get better,' I said. 'Things can only get better.'

'You are wrong. Things will never get better.'

He shook my hand and gave a curt bow.

'Goodnight, my young friend,' he said. 'Remember what I said. I will leave you now. I will go to the brothel.'

That winter I sent Utz a Christmas card and got a postcard in return – of the tomb-slab of Tycho Brahé – hoping that when I next returned to Prague I would call him.

During the months that followed, as the world watched the activities of Comrade Dubček, I tried to imagine Utz's reaction to the events, wondering if he still stuck to his guns: that things would never, ever get better.

As the summer wore on, despite noises in the Soviet press, it seemed less and less likely that Brezhnev would send in the tanks. But one night, as I drove into Paris, the Boulevard Saint-Germain was closed to traffic, and police with riot-shields were pushing back a surge of demonstrators.

The occupation of Czechoslovakia had been completed in a day.

I humped my bag up the stairs of the Hôtel Louisiane and told myself, sadly, that Utz had been right. In December I sent another Christmas card. I never had an answer.

Dr Orlík, on the other hand, was a positive nuisance. Always in a semi-legible scrawl, always on the notepaper of the National Museum, he pestered me for photostats of scientific articles. He commanded me to trace the whereabouts of some mammoth bones in the Natural History Museum. He demanded books: nothing cheap of course, usually monographs published at great expense by American university presses.

One letter informed me of his current project: a study of the house-fly (Musca domestica), as painted in Dutch and Flemish still-lifes of the seventeenth century. My role in this enterprise was to examine every photograph of paintings by Bosschaert, Van Huysum or Van Kessel, and check whether or not there was a fly in them.

I did not reply.

About six years later, towards the end of March 1974, I received from Orlík a black-bordered card on which he had scrawled: 'Our beloved friend Utz is dead . . . '

The word 'beloved' seemed a bit strong: considering I had known Utz for a total of nine and a quarter hours, some six and a half years earlier. All the same, remembering how devoted the two friends were, I sent a short note thanking Orlík for the news, and hoping to share his sorrow.

This produced a flood of even more unreasonable demands. Would I send $1,000 U.S. to help the researches of a poor scholar? Would I agree to sponsor a six-month tour of Western scientific institutions? Would I send forty pairs of socks?

I sent four pairs.

The correspondence dried up.

At the end of last summer I happened to pass through Prague on my way back from the Soviet Union. The mood, especially in smaller cities along the Volga and Don, struck me as exceptionally buoyant. The Soviet education system, I felt, had worked all too well: having created, on a colossal scale, a generation of highly intelligent, highly literate young people who were more or less immune to the totalitarian message.

Prague was infinitely more mournful and gloomy. There were plenty of things in the shops: but the shoppers mooched up and down Wenceslas Square with the faces of a people disgusted with itself for having, if temporarily, lost hope. The works of the 'Prag-Deutsch Schriftsteller', Franz Kafka, were unavailable in the bookstores. Monuments likely to be the focus of national sentiment – the Týn Church or St Vitus's Cathedral – were closed for reconstruction. Their façades had vanished under a blight of rusty scaffolding – although very few workmen could be seen.

It was impossible to drive anywhere without being blocked by a 'road up' sign. The entire city – labyrinthine at the best of times – had been turned into a labyrinth of culs-de-sac. I had the impression of a mercantile city in mourning, not so much for its lost prosperity as the loss of its European role. It was a city at the end of its tether.

I am being unfair. Everywhere in Prague there were signs that the Czechs were uncrushable.

I think it was Utz who first convinced me that history is always our guide for the future, and always full of capricious surprises. The future itself is a dead land because it does not yet exist.

When a Czech writer wishes to comment on the plight of his country, one way open to him is to use the fifteenth-century Hussite Rebellion as a metaphor. I found in Prague Museum this text describing the Hussites' defeat of the German Knights:

'At midnight, all of a sudden, frightened shouting

was heard in the very centre of the large forces of Edom who had put up their tents along three miles near the town of Žatec in Bohemia; in the distance of ten miles from Cheb. And all of them fled from the sword, driven out by the voice of falling leaves only, and not pursued by any man . . .'

As I scribbled this in my notebook, I seemed to hear again Utz's nasal whisper: 'They listen, listen, listen to everything but . . . they *hear* nothing!'

He had, as usual, been right. Tyranny sets up its own echo-chamber; a void where confused signals buzz about at random; where a murmur or innuendo causes panic: so, in the end, the machinery of repression is more likely to vanish, not with war or revolution, but with a puff, or the voice of falling leaves . . .

I was staying at the Hotel Yalta. Among the guests there was a French reporter on the trail of a Peruvian terrorist. 'Many terrorists come to Prague,' he said, 'for facial surgery.'

There was also a party of English 'dissident-watchers': a Professor of Modern History and three literary ladies — who, instead of watching animals in an East African game-park, had come to spy on that other endangered species, the East European intellectual. Was the creature still at large? What should one feed it? Would it compose some suitable words to help the anti-Communist crusade?

They drank whisky on their credit cards, ate a lot of peanuts, and plainly hoped they were being followed. I hoped that, when they did meet a dissident, they'd get their fingers bitten off.

On the following day, I checked for an Utz in the Prague phone book. There was no one of that name.

I ventured past the sickly stucco medusa-masks above the door of No. 5 Široká Street, past the ranks of overflowing dustbins in the entrance, and rang the bell of the top-floor apartment. Beside the bell-push, I saw the screw-holes where Utz's brass plaque had been.

On the landing below, I tried the bell of the soprano who, twenty years earlier, had appeared in a peony-printed peignoir. She was now a shrivelled old lady in a black, fringed shawl. I said the name 'Utz'. The door flew in my face.

I had got as far as the next floor when the door re-opened and, with a 'Psst!', she called me back.

Her name was Ada Krasová. The apartment was crammed with the mementos of an operatic career.

She had sung Mimi, Manon, Carmen, Aida, Ortrud and Lisa in 'The Queen of Spades'. One photograph showed her as an adorable Jenůfa in a lace peasant blouse. She kept fingering the tortoiseshell combs in her hair. In the kitchen a cat was being sick. There were arrangements of peacock feathers in Chinese vases. The profusion of faded pink satin reminded me of Utz's bedroom.

I came quickly to the point. Did she, by any chance, know what had happened to Utz's porcelains? She gave a little operatic trill, 'Oooh! La! La!' – and shuddered. Obviously she did know, but was not letting on. She gave me the name of a curator at the Rudolfine Museum.

The museum, a grandiose edifice from the 'good old days' of Franz Josef, had been named after the Emperor Rudolf to commemorate his passion for the decorative arts. Along the front façade, there were sculptured bas-reliefs representing various crafts: gem-cutting, weaving, glass-blowing. A pair of grimy sphinxes sat guard over the entrance; burdocks were sprouting through cracks in the steps.

The Museum was shut for 'various reasons' – as it had been shut in 1967. Only one room, on the ground floor, was open for temporary exhibitions. The current show was called 'The Modern Chair' – with student copies after Rietveld and Mondrian, and a display of stacking chairs in fibreglass.

At the reception desk I asked to speak to the curator.

Prague is hardly a stone's throw, culturally, from Dresden. I knew that if I posed as an expert on Meissen porcelain, they would soon call my bluff. So I cooked up a likely tale: I was a historian of the Neapolitan Rococo and was writing a paper on the Commedia dell' Arte figurines of the CapodiMonte factory. I had once seen Mr Utz's lovely group 'The Spaghetti Eater'. Was there any way of knowing where it was?

A subdued female voice on the end of the line murmured, 'I will come down.'

I had to wait ten minutes before a homely, middle-aged woman stepped from the lift. Her head was wrapped in a deep lilac scarf, and there was a wen on her chin. She drew back her lips in a covert smile.

'It would be better,' she said in English, 'if we went outside.'

We strolled along the embankment of the Vltava. The day was cold and drizzly, and the clouds seemed to touch the spire of St Vitus's Cathedral. It was one of the worst summers on record. Mallard drakes were chasing ducks in the shallows. A man was fishing from an inflatable rubber dinghy moored in midstream, with the kittiwakes wheeling round him.

'Tell me,' I broke the silence, 'why is your museum always shut?'

'Why do you think?' She let out a quick, throaty laugh. 'To keep the People out!'

She gave a furtive glance over her shoulder, and asked: 'You have known Mr Utz?'

'I knew him,' I replied. 'Not well. I once spent an evening with him. He showed me the collection.'

'When was that?'

'1967.'

'Oh, I see,' she shook her head forlornly. 'Before our tragedy.'

'Yes,' I said. 'I always wondered what became of the porcelain.'

She winced. She took half a step forward, a full step sideways, and then leaned against the balustrade, apparently uncertain how to phrase her next question:

'Do I think correctly that you know the market of Meissen porcelains? In Western Europe and America?'

'I don't,' I said.

'Then you are not a collector?'

'No.'

'Or a dealer?'

'Certainly not.'

'Then you have not come to Prague to buy pieces?'

'God forbid!'

My answer seemed to disappoint her. I had a presentiment she was going to offer to sell me Utz's porcelains. She exhaled a deep breath before continuing.

'Can you tell me,' she asked, 'have pieces from the Utz Collection been sold in the West?'

'I don't believe so.'

A month or so earlier, I had called on Dr Marius Frankfurter in New York, in his overstuffed apartment a-twitter with Meissen birds. 'Find me the Utz Collection,' he had said, 'and we will make ourselves really rich.'

'No,' I said to the curator. 'If anyone knew, it would

be Utz's old dealer friend, Dr Frankfurter. He said it was a total mystery.'

'Oh, I see!' She looked down at the water. 'So you know Dr Frankfurter?'

'I've met him.'

'Yes,' she sighed, 'it is also a mystery to us.'

'How is that?'

She shuddered, and fumbled with the knot of her scarf: 'All those beautiful pieces . . . ! They have gone . . . How would you say it? . . . Vanished!'

'Vanished?' I could hear the air whistling through my teeth.

'Vanished!'

'After his death? Or before?'

'We do not know.'

Until 1973, the year of Utz's stroke, the museum officials were in the habit of paying routine calls on him: to check that the collection was intact.

The visits seemed to amuse him: especially when one or other of the curators brought a puzzling piece of porcelain, on which to test his expertise. But in July of that year, his right arm paralysed, he agreed to sign a paper confirming that, on his death, the collection would go to the State.

He also agreed to import his 'second' collection from Switzerland: with the proviso that, since the visits now distressed him terribly, they would leave him thereafter in peace. The Director of the Museum, a humane man, consented. Two hundred and sixty-seven objects of porcelain were given special clearance through the customs, and were delivered to Utz's apartment.

The funeral, as we know, began at 8 a.m. on March 10th 1974 – although there was some confusion over the timing of the arrangements. As a result, the Director and three of his staff missed the church service and the burial altogether, and were thirty minutes late for breakfast at the Hotel Bristol.

Two days later, when they kept their appointment at No. 5 Široká Street, no one answered the bell. In exasperation, they called for a man to pick the lock. The shelves were bare.

The furniture was in place, even the bric-à-brac in the bedroom. But not a single piece of porcelain could be found: only dust-marks where the porcelains had been, and marks on the carpet where the animals from the Japanese Palace had stood.

'And the servant?' I asked. 'Surely she must know?'

'But we do not believe her story.'

After breakfast next morning, I asked the concierge to call the National Museum to find out if a Dr Václav Orlík still worked there. The answer came back that Dr Orlík, although officially retired, continued to work in the mornings, in the Department of Palaeontology.

On my way to the Museum I took the precaution of reserving a table for two at the Restaurant Pstruh.

A museum guard conducted me through a maze of passages into a storeroom heaped with dusty bones and stones. Orlík, now white-haired and resembling a Brahmanic sage, was cleaning the encrustation from a mammoth tibia. Behind him, like a Gothic arch, was the jawbone of a whale.

I asked if he remembered me.

'Is it?' he scowled. 'No. It is not.'

'It is,' I said.

He left off scouring the mammoth bone and examined me with a myopic and suspicious glare.

'Yes,' he said. 'I see it now. It is you.'

'Of course it's me.'

'Why you not reply to my letters?'

I explained that, since I was last in Prague, I had married and changed addresses five times.

'I do not believe,' he said flatly.

'I wondered if you'd like to lunch with me?' I said. 'We could go to the Pstruh.'

'We could go,' he nodded doubtfully. 'You could pay?'

'I could.'

'So I will come.'

He made the motion of running a comb through his hair and beard, set his beret at a rakish angle, and pronounced himself ready to leave.

On the way out he left a note saying that he had gone to lunch with a 'distinguished foreign scholar'. We went outside. He walked with a limp.

'I do not think you are distinguished,' he said as he limped along the pedestrian underpass. 'I think you are not a scholar even. But I must say it to them.'

Nothing much had changed at the restaurant. The trout were still swimming up and down their oxygenated tank. The head-waiter – could it really be the same head-waiter? – had grown a balloon-like paunch, and the disagreeable face of Comrade Novotný had been replaced by the equally disagreeable face of Comrade Husák.

I ordered a bottle of light white Moravian wine, and raised my glass to Utz's memory. Tears trickled down the creases of Orlík's cheek, and vanished in the wilderness of his beard. I resigned myself to lunching with a tearful palaeontologist.

'How are the flies?' I asked.

'I have returned to the mammoth.'

'I mean your collection of flies.'

'I have thrown.'

The trout, this time, were available.

'Au bleu, n'est-ce pas?' I tried to imitate Utz's weird French accent.

'Blau!' snapped Orlík, with a loud hoot of laughter.

I leaned across, and asked in a lowered voice:

'Tell me, what happened to the porcelains?'

He closed his eyes, and tilted his head from side to side.

'He has thrown,' he said.

'Thrown?'

'Broken and thrown.'

'He broke them?' I gasped.

'He broke and she broke. Sometimes he broke and she threw.'

'She?'

'The Baroness.'

'What Baroness?'

'His Baroness.'

'I never knew he was married.'

'He was married.'

'Who to?'

'He! He!' Orlík cackled. 'Guess it!'

'How can I guess it?'

'You have met the Baroness.'

'I met no one.'

'You have met.'

'I have not met.'

'You have met.'

'Who was she?'

'His domestic.'

'Oh no! No. I don't believe it . . . Not . . . Not Marta!'

'As you say it.'

'And you're saying she destroyed the collection?'

'I am saying and I am not saying.'

'Where is she now?'

'Gone.'

'Dead?'

'Dead, maybe. Maybe not. She has gone.'

'Out of the country?'

'Not.'

'Where then?'

'Into the country.'

'Where in the country?'

'Kostelec.'

'Where's that?'

'Süd-Böhmen.'

'You say she went back to Southern Bohemia?'

'Maybe. Maybe not.'

'Tell me . . . '

'I cannot tell you,' he whispered, 'in here . . . '

Until the end of lunch, Orlík entertained me with an evocation of the mammoth-hunters who had roamed the tundras of Moravia in the Ice Age.

I paid the bill. We took a taxi to the Vrtba Garden where we sat on one of the terraces, beside a stone urn half-covered with a trailing vine.

Utz married Marta at a civil ceremony one Saturday morning in the summer of 1952, six weeks after returning from Vichy.

It was a dangerous moment. The Gottwald regime had let loose the self-perpetuating witch-hunt that culminated in the Slánsky trial. It was almost impossible for ordinary citizens not to fall into one or other of the categories – bourgeois nationalist, traitor to

the Party, cosmopolitan, Zionist, black-marketeer –
that would land them in prison, or worse.

If you happened to be Jewish and a survivor of the
death-camps, this branded you as a Nazi collabor-
ator.

It was obvious to Utz that he would have to tread
with great circumspection.

One morning, an order came for him to quit the
apartment within two weeks: as a single man, he was
no longer entitled to two rooms, only to one.

So it had come to this! He would be out on the
street, or in some rotting garret with nowhere to store
the porcelains. Marriage was the answer.

At the ceremony Marta was very shy, and very
upset by the red flags in the Old Town Hall. 'The
colour of blood,' she shuddered, as they came out into
the sunlight.

On the following Monday, the newlyweds, arm in
arm, joined the shuffling queue of house-seekers, and
presented their marriage certificate to the bureaucrat
in charge. They put on a drooling show of affection.
The eviction order was cancelled.

Marta gave up her own room, and brought her bag
to No. 5 Široká Street.

I cannot vouch for the authenticity of Utz's title 'baron'. Andreas von Raabe, a friend of mine who lives in Munich, assures me that the Utzes of Krondorf did marry, from time to time, into the minor German nobility. He cannot be certain if they were ever ennobled themselves.

Nor, after my call on Dr Frankfurter in New York, do I believe that Utz's annual pilgrimage to the West was quite so 'pure'. I must have been very naive to think the authorities would let him travel back and forth without a favour in return.

Dr Frankfurter's apartment, as I said, was jammed with Meissen and other German porcelain. It was clear that much of it had belonged to aristocratic families in Czechoslovakia and had been sold off, recently, by the State. The Czechs were always in need of hard currency to finance their various activities: espionage or subversion. I now suspect that the safe-deposit in the Union de Banques Suisses in Geneva was an unofficial shop – with a Mr Utz in charge – through which confiscated works of art were sold.

But I *can* state, categorically, that Utz did have a moustache.

Without the moustache, he might have remained in my imagination another art-collector, of fussy habits and feminine inclinations, whose encounters with women were ambiguous.

With the moustache, he was a relentless lady-killer.

'Of course he had a moustache!' Dr Frankfurter shook with smutty laughter. 'The moustache was the clue to his personality!'

Utz had grown the moustache after his adolescent disappointments in Vienna, and had never looked back. He was not the ineffectual lover I had pictured in Vichy. His entire life had been a successful pursuit of voluminous operatic divas: though, since singers of high opera were too temperamental and too obsessed with their art, he tended to settle for the stars of operetta.

A succession of Merry Widows and Countess Mitzis passed through his bed. And if the usual sources of erotic arousal left him cold, he would be driven to frenzy by the sight of a lower larynx, as the singer threw back her head to hit a high note.

He was an ordinary little man. The secret of his attraction to the divas was his technique – you could call it a trick – of applying the stiff bristles of the moustache to the lady's throat so that, for her, the crescendo of love-making was as ecstatic as the final notes of an aria.

The part played by Marta in all this was a sad one.

She had adored Utz with a hopeless and blinkered passion from the moment he beckoned her into his automobile. Yet realising, with a certain peasant canniness, that to hope would drive her mad, she accepted her position. If she did not enjoy his body in this world, she would, with faith, enjoy his soul in the next.

She prayed and prayed. She went tirelessly to Mass. In the Church of Our Lady Victorious she would weep in front of the Prague Baby Jesus: a greedy infant who appropriated pious ladies' necklaces and had his costume changed, weekly, by nuns.

Once, in an outburst of frustrated maternal passion, she offered to help the nuns undress Him, and was rudely rebuffed.

She dared not confess to Him the extent of her ambitions. She begged forgiveness for her husband's infidelities, and for her role in turning the bedroom of No. 5 Široká Street into 'something like a Polish bordel'.

She had never made love to a man — except for one brutal encounter behind a haystack. Yet she acquired

136

a professional's skill in preparing the bedroom for ladies too proud, or too ashamed, to bring an overnight bag.

She applied her entrepreneurial talents on the black market to acquire scented soap, toilet water, talcum-powder, face-powder, towels, flannels and the assortment of pink crêpe-de-chine négligés that unaccountably went missing from the laundry of diplomatic wives.

Sometimes, Utz's visitor found one of these luxuries too tempting to resist, and would stuff it into her reticule. Marta found it expedient to leave an immediate bait on the bed-table — a lipstick or a pair of nylons — and so preserved her more valuable stocks.

She would cook the dinner and wash the dishes. Then, as Utz began his routine with the Commedia figures and the music of 'Ariadne auf Naxos', she would slip out into the night.

Some nights she spent on the floor of her friend Suzana: a woman who kept a vegetable stall on Havelská Street. There were worse nights at the Central Railway Station, her heart in shreds, crossing herself at the thought of thrashing limbs and pink satin.

Since the queue of ladies became more, not less,

pressing over the years, the number of nights she had to sleep out increased. There was never a hint of reproach on her part. Nor, on his, the least acknowledgement that she had ever been inconvenienced.

She believed that, by marrying her, he had done her all the honour in the world. My impression is that, in her mind, and perhaps even in his, she played the part of a consort who is obliged to witness, with amused condescension, a succession of hysterical mistresses.

After moving into the apartment, she had slept under a quilt on the narrow Mies van der Rohe daybed. But one night, while reliving in a nightmare the horrors of Utz's arrest by the Gestapo, she landed on the floor with a reverberative wallop that set the porcelains clattering on the shelves.

Thereafter, she preferred a kapok-filled camping-mattress that could be rolled out in the hallway: any night intruder would have to tread on her.

I uncovered evidence of Marta's unwavering feud with the tenant of the flat below.

Ada Krasová, in the course of a tumultuous affair with Utz, had used her opera singer's privileges to import a bale of pink satin from Italy, and had decorated his bedroom in the taste of a demimondaine.

She then committed the solecism of installing herself on the floor below and, seriously believing she could outwit Marta, had pinched a bottle of Chanel No. 5. Marta countered this act of kleptomania with a bald statement, 'I shall not be cooking for her.' The lady was never invited again: and when I found her, thirty years later, she was still stewing in rancorous recrimination, among her souvenirs.

I don't know the exact date: but sometime in the mid-Sixties, at a performance of 'Don Carlos', Utz trained his opera glasses on the throat of a singer far younger than his usual prey: a substantial girl with an outstanding tonal range who, as Queen of Spain, had to conceal her golden, hawser-like plait within the folds of a black mantilla.

Next day, on his habitual visit to the opera café, Utz summoned up the courage to address her – and recoiled from her stinging reply: 'Get away, you silly old fool!'

It was a lowering winter day. He had an attack of sinusitis and pink-eye. He glanced into the mirror of a shop-front and, in a moment of extreme disillusion, was forced to revise his image of himself as the eternal lover.

What passed between him and Marta, one can only guess. But, from that day on, she quit the camping-mattress and moved into the bed.

The pink art-silk dressing-gown was the emblem of her victory.

His embittered tone, as we parted in the Old Town Square, was perhaps conditioned by the fact that he and his wife had swapped roles. She was too tactful to make a public show, but was certainly the mistress of the household. Henceforth, if he wanted to go philandering, he would have to philander elsewhere.

She then made the victory complete.

She had been married at an atheistic – not to say pagan – ceremony, and had always felt cheated of her

140

rights. In her mumbled conversations with the Infant of Prague, she confessed to having committed a cardinal sin: sleeping with a man to whom she was unmarried in the sight of God.

One day in April, as she and Utz were spring-cleaning some boxes stored on top of the wardrobe, she opened one containing the white lace veil that had been worn by brides of the Utzes since the eighteenth century.

She laid it out on the pink satin coverlet. She looked at him pointedly. He returned her glance.

Utz and Marta were married in the Church of Saint Nikolaus on an incandescent afternoon of plum blossom and hazy blue skies in the 'Prague Spring' of 1968.

She wore a white suit, with minor sweatstains under the arm-pits, and carried a bouquet of white lilacs and lilies-of-the-valley. The veil, pinned over her head, did not look incongruous. A lock of grey hair fell aslant across her brow.

To the Wedding March from 'A Midsummer Night's

Dream', the priest, in ruffles and a wig, led the procession up the aisle.

They passed the inevitable cleaning woman who removed herself and her bucket into a pew, and waved them on gaily with her mop handle. They passed the pulpit, which was the colour of raspberry ice-cream, and arrived in front of the altar where a mitred statue of St Cyril was lancing a pagan with the butt of his crozier.

The onlookers, their curiosity piqued by the disparate sizes of the bride and groom, were taken aback by the elderly couple who turned defiantly to face them: as well as by the smudge of vermilion lipstick that Marta – using lipstick for the first time – had planted on her husband's temple, being too tall to reach his lips at the moment of the bridal kiss.

The organ poured forth Sigmund Romberg's 'When I'm calling you . . .' and as the pair came out into the sunlight, the crowd assembled on the steps broke into a round of hand-clapping.

Another wedding-party was waiting to go in. The young men wore sprigs of myrtle in their lapels. Marta's sharp eye registered that the girl was pregnant. She cringed at the applause, fearing, perhaps, that they were making fun of her. But the bridegroom, a friendly fine-boned boy, bade the Utzes to join them inside for the service, and afterwards at the Hotel Bristol.

A reception for one couple of newlyweds doubled into a reception for two. The revellers, drunk on tokay, made a number of mocking toasts to the bear at the head of the table.

I am now in a position to add to my account of Utz's funeral.

Between the moment of death and the appearance of the undertaker, Marta had obliterated the porcelain shelves with draperies of black material. She called Orlík from the Museum, and the two sat vigil until the coffin was taken away.

Ada Krasová, meanwhile, conducted her own dirge on the floor below. Women from all over Prague, from Brno, from Bratislava; women who had detested each other, on the operatic stage, and as rivals for Utz's affection, were now united in their hatred of Marta for thwarting them of their final glimpse of the moustache.

They screamed. They hissed. They banged on the door. She was deaf to their entreaties.

On the eve of the entombment, she posted Orlík to guard her exit and entrance, and held a conference on the stairwell in which she informed the grieving women of the arrangements for the next day.

With inspired malice, she told them the service would be held in the Church of Saint Jakob instead of Saint Sigismund; the burial at the Vyšehrad Cemetery instead of the Vinohrady; and that breakfast at the Hotel Bristol – 'to which my beloved husband bade you all attend' – would begin at 9.45 a.m. instead of 9.15.

As a result there were two more hired Tatra limousines shuttling back and forth across Prague in the early hours of that bitter morning: one containing a group of retired operatic divas, the other crammed with officials from the Rudolfine Museum.

These two parties coincided at the entrance to the hotel dining-room at the moment when the widow Utz – having raised her tokay glass 'To the Bear! To the Bear!' – was making her remorseless exit.

Taking her leatherette bag into the ladies' lavatory, she changed out of black into a suit of brown wool jersey. She took a taxi to the Central Station, a train to Ceské Budějovice, and went to stay with her sister who still lived in their native village.

When reconstructing any story, the wilder the chase the more likely it is to yield results.

Acting on a tip from Ada Krasová, who made a number of veiled allusions to the hammering that used to sound from Utz's apartment, I stationed myself on the corner of Široká and Maislova Streets, between one and two of a drizzly Saturday morning, to await the emptying of the dustbins.

In Prague, at least in the older quarters, many citizens have an obsessional relationship with garbage. An apartment building such as Nos 5 and 6 Široká Street – built for prosperous bourgeois before the Great War – retains, in the foyer, the original red and yellow marble facings. But where, in the old days, there might have stood a console with a vase of artificial flowers, now, in these less fastidious times, the visitor is greeted by a platoon of grey, galvanised dustbins, of standard size, and with identical articulated lids.

The garbage trucks of Prague are painted a vivid orange. They have been in service for about fifteen years. As a warning to motorists, they are mounted with revolving orange lights that flash their beams against the surrounding architecture. These lights, and the noise of the vehicles' crushing machinery, are the curse of light sleepers but a source of wonder to insomniacs, who will rise from their beds to watch the scene in the street below.

The dustmen wear orange overalls, with leather aprons to protect them as they roll the bins into the street.

I watched a young man remove the refuse of the kosher restaurant in the Jewish Town Hall before moving on to the Golem Restaurant where, earlier in the day, I had sent back a 'Kalbsfilet jüdischer Art' which was garnished with a slice of ham.

He was an energetic young man with laughing eyes and a mop of curly hair. He performed his task with an air of cheerful bravado. The light lit his face into an orange mask.

His companion was a big black Doberman pinscher, his snout in a basketwork muzzle, who either sat on the passenger seat, or hurtled round the block chasing cats, or lovingly rested his forepaws on his master's shoulders.

Turning into Široká Street, the young man manoeuvred the truck arse-first against the kerb, on the opposite side to the Pinkas Synagogue. Then, having rolled out the dustbins from Nos 4, 5 and 6, he stationed them in groups on the sidewalk.

An orange arm shot forth from the truck; clamped its claws around the lip of the bin; lifted it upside down into the air; and, with a double *chu-unk!* . . . *chu-unk!* . . . jettisoned the contents into the vehicle's belly.

The bin returned to earth with a bang, while from inside the truck came the noise of gnashing, crushing, churning, compressing and the shriek of metal teeth.

The Doberman tried to lick my face but was unable to slide its tongue through the muzzle. The dustman was friendly to the man who had befriended his dog and, to my surprise, spoke English.

What was I doing here?

'I'm a writer,' I said.

'So am I,' he said.

Many of his colleagues were writers, or poets or out-of-work actors. They met on Saturdays to drink in a village near the dump. He gave directions how to get there.

'Ask for Ludvík,' he said.

The village was an oasis of orchards and cottage gardens in a waste of industrial pollution. In a garden of roses and hollyhocks, Ludvík was hosing down his truck.

He took me to the bar where his friends, in overalls of orange and blue, were knocking back tankards of Pilsen beer. Some read newspapers, some played chess. In a quiet corner two men were playing back-gammon. They finished, and turned to greet us.

One of the men was the Catholic philosopher, Miroslav Žítek, who, as I knew from émigré publications, was the author of an essay on the self-destructive nature of Force. He was a broadshouldered man with greying sideburns and an open, pink face. He was smoking a meerschaum pipe. He told me how, in Socialist Czechoslovakia, everyone over the age of sixty had the right to a State pension, providing he had put in the required years of work. He and his friends preferred not to embroil themselves in white-collar squabbles: manual labour was better for the mind.

Žítek had worked as a gardener, street-sweeper

and garbage-collector but, with two years to sixty, he found that kind of work exhausting, and had got a new job. He was a bike-boy.

The job was to take computer-software across Prague, from one computer-centre to another. The software fitted into one of his saddlebags, his philosophical treatise into the other. Whenever he made a delivery, the manager of the centre would set aside a room for him to work in. He would work for three hours. Sometimes, at the end of the day, he read a chapter to an audience of workers.

He had some strong things to say about certain Czech writers in exile who, assuming for themselves the mantle of Bohemian culture, neglected what was happening in Bohemia.

Žítek's backgammon-partner was a man with tremendous biceps and a grinning face latticed with scars. His name was Košík. He had gone to America after '68, to Elizabeth, New Jersey, but had returned because the beer was undrinkable.

It was he who, in 1973 – the year of Utz's first stroke – had done the garbage round in the Old Jewish Quarter. He would thus have emptied Utz's dustbins.

I now come to the most difficult part of my story. Once I took it into my head that the Utz Collection *could* have vanished down the maw of a garbage truck, my temptation was to twist every scrap of evidence in that direction.

Košík answered my questions with amused good humour. But I am doubtful, in retrospect, whether his answers were genuine, or the answers I wanted to hear. I cannot place much reliance on the image he spun for me: that, when clearing the bins of No. 5 Široká Street, he sometimes saw a shadowy figure flattening himself or herself against the back wall of the entrance lobby. One night, he said, a pair of figures appeared at the window of the top floor apartment – and waved.

I felt I was on firmer ground with Košík's second story: here, at least, there was a measure of agreement among his drinking companions.

They agreed that ten or twelve years ago – more maybe – a taxi used to bring an elderly couple to the village for a Sunday afternoon stroll. The man was shorter than the woman, shuffled his feet, and had to be supported on her arm. They would walk along the lane, as far as the wire fence surrounding the dump, and then walk back to the taxi.

I walked along the lane.

The fields were overgrown with ragwort and willow-herb. Factory chimneys were churning clouds of brown smoke in the direction of the city. The sky was tied in a tangle of electric cables.

I came to the fence. A rank of bulldozers stood outside a shed. Beyond lay the dump: an area of raw earth and refuse, with seagulls screaming over it.

I walked back to the village, thinking over the various possibilities.

Had Utz or Marta smuggled the collection abroad? No. Had the museum officials smuggled it abroad? No. Dr Frankfurter would have known. Did Utz destroy his porcelains out of pique? I was doubtful. He loathed museums, but he was not a vindictive man.

But he *was* a joker! I felt it might have appealed to his sense of the ridiculous that these brittle Rococo objects should end up on a twentieth-century trash-heap.

Or was it a case of iconoclasm? Is there, alongside the tendency to worship images – which Baudelaire called 'my unique, my primitive passion' – a counter-tendency to smash them to bits? Do images, in fact, demand their own destruction?

Or was it Marta? Did *she* have the vindictive streak? Did she connect Utz's love of porcelain with his love for opera singers? If so, having got rid of one lot, she might as well rid herself of the other.

151

No. My impression is that none of these theories will work. I believe that, in reviewing his life during those final months, he regretted having always played the trickster. He regretted having wheedled himself and the collection out of every tight corner. He had tried to preserve in microcosm the elegance of European court life. But the price was too high. He hated the grovelling and the compromise – and in the end the porcelains disgusted him.

Marta had never given in. She had never once lowered her standards, never lost her craving for legitimacy. She had stayed the course. She was his eternal Columbine.

My revised version of the story is that, on the night of their wedding in church, she emerged from the bathroom in her pink art-silk dressing-gown and, unloosing the girdle, let it slide to the floor and embraced him as a true wife. And from that hour, they passed their days in passionate adoration of each other, resenting anything that might come between them. And the porcelains were bits of old crockery that simply had to go.

The village of Kostelec lies close to the Austrian border, near the watershed between the Danube and the Elbe. The wheatfields have been invaded by biblical 'tares': but the cornflowers, the poppies, knapweed, scabious, and larkspur make one rejoice in the beauty of a European countryside as yet unpoisoned by selective weedkillers. On the edge of the village there are water-meadows and, beyond, there is a lake where carp are raised, half-encircled with a stand of pines.

The houses of the village have red-tiled roofs, and their walls are freshly washed with ochre and white. The women plant geraniums in their window-boxes. On the village green, there is a well-tended chapel with a tiny dome.

Beside the chapel there is the base of a monument which once would have borne the double K's — Kaiserlich und Königlich — of the Dual Hapsburg Monarchy. It now supports a rusty, lopsided contraption commemorating a Soviet foray into space.

A storm was passing. The thunderheads rolled away, and a rainbow arched over the water-meadows.

The sun illuminated gardens of yellow rudbeckia, purple phlox and banks of white shasta daisies.

I unlatched a wicket-gate. A snow-white gander flapped towards me, craning his neck and hissing. An old peasant woman came to the door. She wore a flowered housecoat, and a white scarf low over her forehead. She frowned. I murmured a word or two and her face lit up in an astounded smile.

And she raised her eyes to the rainbow and said, 'Ja! Ich bin die Baronin von Utz.'